INNOCENT PEOPLE

To: Nick Karegeannes
with Sincere Apprecieateio
for your Outstanding
Service.

From: Salem School.
5/26/2006

INNOCENT PEOPLE

A Novel

by

Linda-Jamilah Kolocotronis

ISBN: 1-58597-209-6

Library of Congress Control Number: 2003111193

A division of Squire Publishers, Inc.
4500 College Blvd.
Leawood, KS 66211
1/888/888-7696
www.leatherspublishing.com

CONTENTS

PREFACE

On the morning of September 11, 2001, I was a social studies teacher at the Islamic School of Kansas City. I had first period free, and was waiting for my second period class to arrive when the language arts teacher called me into her room. She had been listening to news on the radio during her free period, and learned of the attacks. I had a few minutes to digest the information before the seventh and eighth grade boys arrived in my classroom. I decided to tell them what had happened, as much as I knew at that point. We had a brief discussion, then we read the Qur'an together. Some boys went to find information on the internet. One of the seventh-graders, Hassan, stood up to pray. Then, one by one, parents came to pick up their children. School was closed for the rest of the week.

All of the characters in this novel, with the exception of Hassan and Jean, the librarian, are fictional. Some characters are loosely based on people I know, while others are simply figments of the writer's imagination.

All of the major events resulting from 9/11 that are mentioned in this book — the arrest and deportation of Pakistani men, harassment of girls wearing scarves in public, detention based on mistaken identity — did occur. In most cases, I have not personally known someone who was involved in these events. However, I have read and heard accounts from those were who involved.

On September 11, 2001, the entire nation was devastated by the attacks on our soil, and we are still being affected in many ways. *Innocent People* is the story of one American Muslim woman, and how the attacks affected her and her family.

SADIA'S FRIENDS AND FAMILY

Salahuddin .... My husband of twenty-one years

Muhammad .... My oldest son, a senior in high school

Sadeq .... My sixteen-year-old son

Adam .... My twelve-year-old son

Yusuf .... My ten-year-old son

Amin .... My youngest, who's in first grade now

Maryam .... My best friend for almost eighteen years

Musa .... Maryam's husband (the strong, silent type)

Mrs. Robinson ..... The sweet older lady who lives next door

Imran .... A very intelligent young man who teaches social studies at the Islamic School

Khadijah .... Another good friend. She's married to Imran.

Yaqub .... Salahuddin's right-hand man at the restaurant

Ali .... Owner of the local Muslim market

Uthman .... A chemistry professor. He has three kids in our school. His wife is Asma.

Asma .... The fifth grade teacher. We've been casual friends for many years.

Hussein .... One of our friends. His kids go to the Islamic school.

Asiya .... Hussein's wife. She's sweet, and a little shy.

CHAPTER ONE

A Silent Night

THE HOUSE IS quiet, and quiet is good. There are no pounding footsteps made by boys running up the stairs. There are no loud voices, raised in momentary anger or childhood glee. No doors are squeaking and no video games are beeping. At last, the house is quiet.

Salahuddin is downstairs in the living room, watching the news. A moment ago I kissed him on the cheek and headed up to our room. On my way down the hall I stop to peek in at my three youngest. Amin is sleeping peacefully in the toddler bed, which is really too small for him. Brown curls frame his still-babyish features, and when he sleeps his hands sometimes still form partial fists. My sweet baby boy, who only hours ago was screaming and jumping off the couch, now breathes softly and slowly, occasionally giggling in his sleep.

I glance over at the bunk beds on the other side of the room. Yusuf is stretched out on the lower bunk, left arm and left leg flung carelessly over the side as usual. Adam is reading in his upper perch.

"Lights out soon, Adam."

"Okay, Mom."

I close the door softly and continue down the hall. On the way to my own refuge I must pass the teen hangout that is otherwise known as Muhammad's and Sadeq's room. I press my ear to the door, half afraid that they'll think I'm spying on them. The TV is playing softly — a late night sitcom that I prefer they didn't watch. Maybe they need to

1

know that someone is checking on them. I rap lightly on the door.

"Don't stay up too late, boys."

"We won't," says Muhammad.

"Is your homework done?"

"Almost," says Sadeq.

They probably haven't even started it yet. "Okay. Well, get your homework done and get to bed. Do you hear me, boys?"

"Yes, Mom," each replies, not too loudly or enthusiastically.

Feeling satisfied that I've fulfilled my parental duty, I make my way finally to the master bedroom. Master bedroom is an apt description, I think. This is the sanctuary of the king and queen, a place to take refuge after another day with our unruly subjects.

After getting ready for bed I take a moment to look at the outfit I've chosen to wear for my interview tomorrow. The skirt is black and narrow, going all the way down to my ankles. The silk top, one that Salahuddin bought for me in Singapore, is a swirl of white and green. I've always liked this outfit, and usually receive compliments when I wear it. Hopefully it will be impress my future boss.

I thought that I would stay awake until Salahuddin comes up, but the quiet is so relaxing. I lay my head on the pillow, and soon begin to dream of the wonderful day ahead.

CHAPTER TWO

A Normal Morning

"SADIA, YOU NEED to get up to pray." Salahuddin shakes my shoulder gently. I hear him, but it takes me another moment to remember my life — my name, my home, my family — as I pull myself out of my dreams.

Amin is knocking at my bedroom door. "Mom, I can't find my other shoe." He's probably dressed and all ready to go, except for that shoe, of course. At least one of my kids is a morning person, like their father.

"Just a minute, Amin. Mama needs to get herself ready."

"But I need my shoe."

"Wait a minute, Amin. I'll be there soon."

I slowly pull myself out of bed, make my ablutions and say my morning prayers in a corner of my bedroom. It's so late, I'm sure Salahuddin and the older boys have already prayed.

I open my bedroom door, and Amin is still there. "Mom, I can't find my other shoe," he repeats.

"Did you look on the back porch?"

"No." He stands there, looking at me as if his shoe will magically appear in my hand.

"Well, why don't you look on the back porch. Maybe it's underneath something."

"Okay." He skips down the hall and runs down the stairs, happily headed on the special mission to find his lost shoe.

I follow him, slowly and sleepily. On the way I pass Sadeq, who's standing outside the bathroom door.

"Mom, can you tell Muhammad to hurry up. He's been

in there for about an hour already."

I doubt Muhammad has been in there that long, but I shout my reminder, "Muhammad, hurry up. Your brothers have to use the bathroom, too."

The kitchen is quiet. Salahuddin is almost finished eating breakfast, and Yusuf is pouring milk on his cereal. Amin walks in from the back porch, missing shoe in hand.

"You were right, Mom. How did you know?"

"Experience," I say. He looks puzzled. "I've been a mom for a long time."

"Amin, go on out to the car. Yusuf, hurry up and finish eating. What's taking those boys of yours so long?" Salahuddin is anxious to begin his day.

"Well, the last time I checked, Muhammad was in the bathroom and Sadeq was waiting for him to finish." I have to stop to do a little mental math. Who's missing? "Adam. Has anyone seen Adam yet this morning?"

"No," says Salahuddin, "but you need to make sure he's up and ready. That Adam has been late every day since school started."

"Adam." I call up the stairs. Sadeq is still waiting in the hall. "Sadeq, have you seen Adam yet this morning?"

"No, he's probably still asleep."

Yes, he probably is. "Sadeq, could you go wake him up?"

Muhammad finally emerges from the bathroom, and Sadeq quickly heads in. "I've got to get ready, Mom." He shuts the door.

"Never mind, I'll do it," I say, to no one in particular. The stairs are quite steep at this time of the morning, and by the time I get to the top I'm ready to crawl back in bed myself.

I knock on the door. "Adam, are you awake?"

His alarm clock is beeping, but there's no sound of movement. I open the door and look up at the top bunk. Adam is still sleeping soundly. He mutters, "Dragon ... get you." It's going to be hard to wake him up. I should have made him turn off his light and go to sleep earlier last night. He probably stayed up half the night reading that book.

"Adam." I fold back his favorite blue blanket and gently shake his shoulder. "Hurry up. Your father's waiting."

He groans. "Okay, Mom, I'm coming." He opens his eyes briefly, then closes them again.

"Come on, Adam. You'll be late for school again." I have to go check on the other boys, but I pause a moment before leaving the room to look at my middle son — in that moment before he became just another active twelve-year-old boy. With his dark eyes and thick black hair, he looks like a miniature of Salahuddin. His imagination and stubbornness show that he's definitely mine, too.

I have to make sure Amin ties his shoes properly, remind Yusuf to brush his hair and get Sadeq away from the bathroom mirror. I prefer sending the boys off with a nice hot breakfast in the morning, but most days I'm happy that someone thought to invent cold cereal and the toaster. I wonder if it was a woman.

Finally Amin, Yusuf and Muhammad are all ready and headed for the car. Sadeq is coming out of the bathroom, dressed and headed for the stairs. There's still one missing. "Adam," I call up the stairs, "your father is ready to leave. You'd better get moving!"

I hear him shut his bedroom door and stumble towards the bathroom. "Man," says Sadeq, "you're really late today. I bet you get yelled at all the way to school." Sadeq runs down the stairs as he speaks.

Salahuddin honks the horn several times. Finally, Adam emerges from his room, dressed but barefoot, and heads downstairs.

"What about your shoes and socks? Have you prayed yet?"

"It's still pretty warm, Mom. I'll put my stuff on in the car. I'll pray when I get to school."

"Okay," I sigh. "Borrow Sadeq's comb and brush your hair in the car, too." I don't know if he hears me as he slams the door.

At last, the house is quiet again. I take a deep breath, savoring the moment. I eat my own toaster-enhanced breakfast and quickly clean up the kitchen before sitting down to enjoy the silence.

I try to read, but just can't concentrate. All I can think of is my job interview this afternoon. I'm tempted to check my outfit again, but I resist. It's been so long since I've been out in the real world that I don't know how regular working people dress. I keep trying to imagine how the interview will go.

"So, Mrs. Abdullah. Tell me about your job experience."

"Well, sir, I haven't actually held a regular job for the last eighteen years. Raising my sons, you know. I can make a pumpkin pie from scratch, though, and I can tackle any stain known to man. I did have a 3.75 grade point average in college. I majored in psychology and graduated with honors."

"That's nice, Mrs. Abdullah, but I'm afraid your skills are a little too outdated for our organization. Good luck with your job search."

What a bad dream! I shake myself. Okay, Sadia, be positive. You're raising five boys. You've helped Salahuddin get his restaurant off the ground. You've served on countless committees. You've been a room mother for thirteen years. You're smart. They need you. I'm starting to feel better.

The phone rings, shaking me from my quiet world.

"Assalaamu alaikum, girl. How you doing?"

"Walaikum assalaam, Maryam. I'm fine, I guess. Just a little nervous about this interview."

"Oh, you'll knock their socks off."

"I sure hope so. What's going on with you?"

"Musa and I have been talking about going down to Texas to visit Laila and her husband for a couple weeks or so. I sure miss that little boy of hers. Did I tell you she's pregnant again?"

"No. Congratulations! This will make, um, seven grand-children?"

"Yes, seven of them. I sure love being a grandma. I get to spoil them all I want."

Maryam and I talk for a few more minutes, mostly about kids and grandkids. I can hear the TV in the background. Musa always likes to start his day with "Good Morning, America."

Suddenly, Maryam gasps. "Oh, my God!"

I hear Musa's deep voice in the background. "What the …"

"What is it, Maryam?"

"Turn on your TV, Sadia. I don't know what to say. Just turn on your TV. I'll talk to you later. Assalaamu alaikum." She hangs up.

"Walaikum assalam," I say to the dial tone. Maryam is always so calm. What's going on?

I turn on the TV, and I see it. One of the towers of the World Trade Center is burning. Why? What happened?

Charles Gibson is on, trying to explain, when it happens again. I see it. A plane flies into the other tower, I think. A plane flies into the tower? How can that be?

I sit down. My first thought is, this must be an accident. My second thought is, please don't let it be Muslims. This becomes a prayer. "Please, Allah, please don't let Muslims be involved."

I continue to watch, mesmerized by the images of destruction. People are running. They say that some are jumping to their deaths. I become lost in the terror of the moment.

The phone rings, and I jump. It's Salahuddin. "Salahuddin, I'm so glad you called. Do you know what's happened?"

"Yes, Sadia, I know. I'm going to pick up the boys from school. We'll be home soon, insha Allah."

"Be careful. Please be careful."

"I will. I'll see you soon." He hangs up, and I'm alone again in my terror.

In a moment of crisis you can think of the strangest

things. I think of slurpees. I remember, now, that I had promised the boys we'd go for slurpees after school. I hoped, actually, that it would be a small celebration for landing my new job. I guess now, though, there will be no celebration.

In fact, I guess, there will be no job. Not even the interview. The assumption is already being made, coast to coast, that Muslims are behind the terror I see on my screen. There is no way that I would get that job. I don't even feel like leaving the house. I think vaguely about calling in to cancel, but at the moment I can't get up from my front row seat to disaster. My guess is that they probably won't even miss me.

I continue to watch as catastrophe rules on national television. After a while, I become anxious about Salahuddin and the boys. They should be home by now. I pull myself away from the TV screen to look out the front window for our blue minivan.

What I see looks so strange, because everything is the same. There are no burning buildings or screaming people. Mrs. Robinson is out watering her flowers, as usual — she must not have heard the news yet. The Browns' dog is barking. The mail truck is parked up the street, and the mailman is calmly making his rounds. The morning newspaper is still out on our lawn. In the excitement of getting the kids off to school, thinking about my job interview and watching terrorist attacks, I had completely forgotten about it. It doesn't seem worth reading now. There could never be news as important, as urgent, as what is happening before my eyes, courtesy of network television.

I leave the neighborhood scene of deceptive calm and go back to sit on the couch in my living room, in my small Midwestern town, watching the disaster unfold one thousand miles away.

CHAPTER THREE

Catching My Breath

FINALLY, I HEAR noises and voices in the driveway. My family is home. They're safe. By the time they walk in, I am sitting on the couch again, stunned by the news of still more airline crashes — one in Pennsylvania and the other at the Pentagon. I want to go to my family, but I can't pull myself away.

"Assalaamu alaikum, Sadia. Sadia, we're home."

I manage to pull myself out of the trance. "Oh, oh, I'm so glad that you made it home safely." I hug each of them, tightly. Wives and mothers in New York will be mourning family members today, but at least mine are safe. I reach for Salahuddin. "I've been so worried."

"We're home now, alhamdulillah."

Amin looks up at me. He can probably see the redness in my eyes and hear the tension in my voice. "What's wrong, Mama?"

I put on a false smile, and wipe my eyes. "Nothing's wrong, Amin. Mama's just happy to see you." I hug him again, enjoying the smell of sweet innocence, then look up. "Tell you what, Amin. Why don't you go to your room with Yusuf? You two can play with your new toys."

"Okay," says Amin. He slips away from my arms and runs to his room to play with the latest movie-related action figures. Yusuf stays behind.

"Do I have to go, Mom? I want to know what's going on. Why did we come home so early? Why is everyone so upset? Sr. Asma didn't tell us anything, just that we wouldn't have any more classes today."

I sit down on the couch and gently tell Yusuf about the planes. As I finish my explanation, the scene is replayed on the TV. Yusuf watches in wonder.

"Wow, cool! Was that real?"

"Yes, Yusuf, and it isn't cool. Thousands of people have been killed. I'm just so glad to have you boys here safe at home."

"Who did it? Was it Muslims?"

"I don't know, Yusuf. We'll just have to wait and see."

"I guess I'll go play with Amin now." He pretends to be flying a plane as he walks down the hall.

I am about to turn my attention back to the TV when I see Adam standing in the doorway. "Come here, Adam. How are you doing?"

"I'm scared, Mom." He comes and sits next to me on the couch.

"It sure is scary. Did your teachers tell you about it at school?"

"Yes, Br. Imran did. When we came into the room for social studies class, he was just sitting at his desk, not saying anything. After a while Hassan asked him what was wrong, and he told us. He also said that Muslims will probably be blamed. Is that true?"

"Yes, Adam, I'm afraid it is. Muslims have been accused of doing terrible things in the past, and I'm afraid that it's going to happen again. I don't know what's going on yet. I guess no one does."

"After Br. Imran told us about it, we got together to read Qur'an. Hassan stood up by himself and prayed. Some of the guys went on the internet to see what they could find out. It was kind of weird." Adam pauses. "Mom, Baba was really mad at me for being late. I'm sorry. I'll try to do better."

"I know you will, Adam. Why don't you go play with Yusuf and Amin now. We still have a couple of hours before lunch."

"Can I watch TV with you and Baba? I want to know what's going on."

"Are you sure, Adam? It's awfully sad, and scary."

"That's okay. I really want to know."

Adam sits there on the couch with Salahuddin and me as we watch the tragedy unfold. Salahuddin is quiet, as usual. I'm not so strong. Predictably, Muslims are named as the culprits several times during the next hour. Fear and anxiety rise in my chest. I can't stay silent.

"How can they just start accusing Muslims? Don't they know what Islam stands for? Muslims couldn't have done this!"

Salahuddin gives me a look. "Calm down, Sadia. Just watch for now and see what they have to say. It's still early."

Salahuddin almost never gets upset. It's his culture — well, partly anyway. He's from Singapore, where they have so much self-control that they don't even chew gum. Sometimes he's so calm that it drives me crazy. He can't understand why I get upset. I keep reminding him that I'm half Greek, but he still doesn't get it.

I try to stay quiet, listening to them go on and on about the Muslim terrorists. Finally I can't stand it any more. "I'll go make lunch now." I don't think Salahuddin even notices when I leave the room.

I call everyone into the kitchen for a lunch of canned soup and grilled cheese sandwiches. This is not the time for real cooking. I do insist that they all come eat at the kitchen table. Only Yusuf and Amin come willingly. Everyone else must be dragged in.

Lunch is mostly quiet. Muhammad and Sadeq eat as quickly as possible so that they can go back to the solitude of their room. Salahuddin and Adam are distracted, probably thinking about all the news they're missing during this enforced family time. Only Amin chatters away, oblivious to the cloud that hangs over our heads. Most of the time he just talks to himself, making up stories about superheroes who always win over evil.

I make Adam and Yusuf help me clean up after lunch. Amin hangs around and helps a little, too. As we are finishing up, Amin asks, "Are we going to get slurpees now? Remember, you promised."

What should I say to him? I hesitate. "We can't go get slurpees today, Amin. We need to stay home."

"But why, Mama? It's not raining. Why can't we go?"

Before I can say anything, Yusuf answers. "It's because some bad guys crashed some planes into some buildings and they think that Muslims did it. We have to hide out or they might get us!"

Amin runs to me and hides his face in my long skirt. "Mom, Yusuf's lying."

I kneel down and put my arms around Amin. "No, Amin, he's right. Something bad did happen today. They're not coming to get us," I glance at Yusuf, "but it's better if we just stay home for now."

Amin begins to cry softly. "I'm scared, Mama."

I hold Amin for several minutes. "It's okay, Amin. Mama's here. You're safe. I promise." I can't tell him that I'm scared, too.

After a while, Amin stops crying and becomes calmer. "Can we go get slurpees tomorrow then, Mom?"

"I don't know, Amin. We'll just have to see."

He thinks about that for a while. Finally he says, "Can I go play again?"

"Sure you can." I watch as he runs down the hall.

I go to the living room and find Salahuddin and Adam sitting motionless, their gazes fixed on the TV. They're still sitting this way half an hour later when the phone rings.

"Hello?"

"Assalaamu alaikum, Sadia. This is Yaqub. I need to speak with Salahuddin. It's important."

Yaqub is Salahuddin's assistant manager at the restaurant. Salahuddin opened the restaurant, Malaccan

Muslim Delight, sixteen years ago. In the early days I helped out as much as little Muhammad and Sadeq allowed. But then along came Adam, Yusuf and Amin, so Salahuddin hired Yaqub to take my place. I was happy he did.

I call Salahuddin to the phone. He mostly listens. I hear him say, "I'll be right there." He doesn't look happy.

"What's wrong?"

"Someone called in a bomb threat to the restaurant. Yaqub has already called the police, but I'd better go check it out. The police may want to talk to me, too."

"Well, please be careful."

"I will. Hopefully I won't be gone long." He gives me a kiss on the cheek and heads out the door.

I sigh. It happened only this morning, but already I'm wondering how long it will take for life to get back to normal.

CHAPTER FOUR

Feeling Threatened

SALAHUDDIN COMES BACK a few hours later. There were no problems at the restaurant, just the threat. Still, he had to call the police, wait for them to come and file a report.

"The police said they will keep an eye on the restaurant while they are on patrol. I guess that's all they can do for now."

Soon after Salahuddin comes home, we get a phone call from the school secretary. Did I mention that all my kids go to an Islamic school?

"Assalaamu alaikum, Sadia. How are you holding up?"

"We're doing okay, alhamdulillah. What about you? Are there any problems at the school?"

"That's why I'm calling. We've already received a few phone threats. The principal and the school board have decided to close the school for the rest of the week, just to be on the safe side. The police will set up a patrol around the school to keep an eye on the building. Hopefully things will be a little calmer by Monday."

"I sure hope so."

"Oh, and we're having a meeting for parents on Sunday at 4:00 to talk about security. I hope you and your husband can come."

"We'll be there, insha Allah."

"I have to call some more parents. I hope to see you on Sunday."

Yes, I hope so. We'll be there, I said. Salahuddin will be

there. I should have said that. But can I go, too? Will it be safe for me to leave the house with my scarf on? I haven't left the house without a scarf for over twenty years. Would this be enough to make me change my mind?

The next few days pass quickly. I have very little time to myself. Most of my time is spent fixing meals, cleaning up and giving hugs (except for my oldest boys, who think they are way too old for hugs!).

In my rare quiet moment I think about the irony of the situation. Most Americans are terrified that there will be more terrorist attacks. I'm terrified, too, but not just of terrorist attacks. I'm also terrified of other Americans. The news commentators speak about the grief and shock, but they talk mostly about the anger. My fellow American citizens are angry, and some want to take action. These emotions are normal but, unfortunately for my Muslim sisters and me, there are a few crazies out there who are anxious to turn anger into revenge, and they can't tell the difference between a bona fide terrorist and a mom with a headscarf.

When my mother calls from California on Wednesday, she validates my fears. "You'd better stay inside, Sally. You just don't know what people might do these days."

My mother still calls me by the name she chose when she saw the soft tufts of yellow hair on my newborn head. She said I looked just like the girl in the reading book. When I became a Muslim I took an Arabic name, and that's the name I generally use — because I don't want people to think of me as just a cute little girl in a reading book. I like Sadia. It means happy and, well, I try.

During these days of isolation, I become increasingly concerned about the attitudes of my two oldest. The younger three seem to be managing, each in his own way. Amin continues to play, safe in the knowledge that his parents will always protect him. Yusuf keeps asking questions — about the planes, the hijackers, everything. Adam is worried, I can tell, but he continues to read his books and play with his younger brothers while keeping a watchful eye on the news.

My two oldest, though, are another story altogether. They spend most of their time in that room. I do check up on them once in a while, just to remind them that we're still here. I hear the TV, but I know they're not watching the news. Once Muhammad actually opened the door, and I got a glimpse of the inner chamber. They're watching action videos. I guess it's more comfortable to live in a world where Jet Li and Jackie Chan always beat the bad guys and innocent people don't get hurt.

I've always tried to be an understanding mother, but by Thursday I'm getting tired of their indifference. At dinner, I finally challenge them. "Boys, you don't seem to even care about what's going on. Don't you realize what a tragedy this is?"

"Sure, Mom," Sadeq answers, "but it's not like we can do anything about it."

"Yeah, Mom," Muhammad adds, "people get killed and Muslims get blamed. What else is new?"

I shake my head, and sigh. "I guess we've come a long way from the days of Flower Power."

"What's that?" asks Amin. "Do flowers have special powers to fight the bad guys?"

"No, Amin, it's nothing like that. Back when I was a teenager, way back in the Stone Age," Salahuddin chuckles at this, "the young people cared about what was going on in the world. There were protests against the war in Vietnam and, a few years later, a push to remove a corrupt president from office. We cared about the environment and wildlife. We wanted to eliminate poverty. We thought we were going to change the world."

"But you didn't, did you?" says Sadeq. He's smirking. I feel like smacking him, but I never hit my children. This might be a good time to start, I think briefly.

Sadeq can see the irritated look on my face. I wonder if he knows how much danger he's in. "I'm sorry. I just meant, you and your friends worked so hard, but nothing changed, did it?"

I have to think about that one for a minute. "Well, new standards were implemented to cut down on pollution. Laws were created to protect the rights of consumers. Nixon was forced to resign. The U.S. did finally withdraw the troops from Vietnam. The world sure isn't perfect now, but maybe it would have been worse if we hadn't tried to change things."

"Yeah, maybe," says Muhammad. "Anyway, there is one thing I'd really like to change. They cancelled the pro football games this weekend. Can you believe it?"

"I know," Sadeq adds. "It's not like planes are going to crash into the stadiums."

"Yeah," says Muhammad. "I don't know what I'm going to do on Sunday without football."

A variety of mom phrases pop into my head. You could clean your room, straighten up the garage, help out at the restaurant, spend more time studying. I'm trying to decide which one to use for the greatest effect when Salahuddin comes into the conversation.

"I agree. That's a terrible thing," he says, with a serious expression and a wink in my direction. "I can help you with all that spare time. Why don't you clean up around the house, help out at the restaurant and do your homework? You could do it as a form of protest." Triple play. I'm impressed.

"Yes, Baba," says Muhammad. He winces.

Sadeq jabs Muhammad with his elbow and whispers, "Man, you should have stayed quiet." They are quiet for the rest of the meal. They know that their father will follow through with his promise

On Friday Salahuddin takes Muhammad and Sadeq with him to make the weekly congregational prayers. While they're gone, I'm glued, once again, to the TV. Commentators are talking about how the alleged hijackers spent their last night at a bar.

When Salahuddin comes home, I begin my ranting. "Can you believe that? These men were supposed to be Muslims. They said they were carrying out the attacks as a form of jihad. We already know how wrong they were on that count, killing innocent people and all, but now look. They spent their last night in a bar. How can they even call themselves Muslims? They just fooled around, did whatever they wanted and left the rest of us holding the bag!"

Salahuddin is used to my rants. He waits until I've settled down, then gives me something new to think about.

"During the khutbah today, the imam said that the hijackers still haven't been positively identified. They may not even have been Muslim. There are a lot of theories going around right now. Just take some time to think about it before you get too upset again."

They might not have been Muslims? Who were they? Salahuddin can't tell me. All he can say is that not all of the facts are known yet.

The fog of the last four days begins to lift. More than three thousand people are still dead, and we've learned that several hundred of the victims were Muslims. It was a terrible, horrible thing, but I've felt that there was no time to grieve. I've just been so busy worrying about how this will affect Muslims, here in this country and throughout the world. Now, maybe, I can have some time to be sad, and even a little angry.

It really tore up my stomach when I saw the pictures of the so-called hijackers in the newspaper yesterday. Some of those boys weren't much older than Muhammad. Oh, I hope they didn't do it.

Maybe the newspaper was wrong. Maybe the hijackers weren't Muslims. As terrible, as tragic as these events are, I start to feel hopeful. Maybe there will be an end to this nightmare.

CHAPTER FIVE

My Bodyguards

FOR FOUR DAYS I have stayed inside my house, daring only to peek out the windows. I let the younger boys play outside in the yard, but I felt that I needed to check on them constantly. Salahuddin and the older boys have gone out, of course, but it was easier for them because they aren't easily identifiable as Muslims. I have actually thought about removing my scarf because of the danger. I gave it deep consideration for all of thirty seconds.

Until Friday afternoon, I was determined to stay in my house for as long as it took for things to get back to normal — days, weeks, maybe even months or years. I have heard stories of women with agoraphobia who hadn't left their houses for ten or twenty years. If they could do it, I guess I could, too.

When Salahuddin told me that Muslims may not have committed the attacks, it changed my outlook. My relief is unfounded, of course, because most of the people in the world still believe that Muslims were behind it, and they may have been. Still, this new piece of information, while not verified, makes me feel more optimistic than I've felt since I woke up last Tuesday morning.

When I wake up on Saturday, I am determined. The day is fresh and new, and I intend to take advantage of it. I wait until Salahuddin finishes his breakfast before approaching him. I speak fast, quickly laying out all my points.

"Salahuddin, I'm going crazy staying inside this house. I need some sunshine. I need to interact with people who don't need their shoes tied and don't prefer a video game over conversation with me."

He looks up from his newspaper. I have his attention. I continue. "We need some groceries. We're almost out of cereal, with the boys being home all week, and milk and bread and lots of other things. I don't even need to go by myself. I can take Muhammad and Sadeq with me, as my bodyguards. I really need to get out of this house."

Salahuddin puts down the front page section of the paper and looks at me. "Can't you just stay home a little longer? I'll be happy to go to the store for you. Just write a list."

Okay, it's time for the heavy ammunition. "This is my country. I have to find out what's going on in the outside world. If I don't go out now, then when? Besides, I'll have Muhammad and Sadeq with me in case there's a problem."

"Sadia, you know I'm not trying to make you a prisoner."

"I know. But do you remember that job interview I was supposed to go to? I had to sacrifice that, but I'm not willing to sacrifice my whole life."

"I'm not asking for your whole life. Just a few more days."

The discussion is becoming heated. I don't want an argument, just a few hours of freedom. I take a deep breath before my next response.

"Salahuddin, we've been married for twenty-one years. You should know me by now. Back when we got married I told you that I wasn't going to just sit around the house all my life." I pause, struck by sudden inspiration. "Besides, didn't you tell me stories about your grandmother going out during the Japanese occupation? That was a whole lot more dangerous."

He's silent for a moment, and then he laughs. "My mother told me I was going to have trouble when I decided to marry an American woman. You're not going to take no for an answer, are you?"

"No, but your grandmother wasn't an American."

"No, but she was just as stubborn as you are." He pulls me on his lap, and we kiss. "Just be careful. If anything happens to you, I'll have to go back home and let my mother choose my next wife."

I decide to go after lunch. When we're finished eating, Salahuddin talks to the boys.

"Your mother is determined to go grocery shopping. I'm depending on you two to be her bodyguards."

"Okay," says Sadeq. "Do I get to beat anybody up?"

"Only if necessary. Now, go on. Have a good time."

While Salahuddin rounds up the younger boys to do the dishes, I head out with my bodyguards. Muhammad, a senior in high school, is nearly six feet tall. Sadeq, who's sixteen, isn't quite as tall, but he still towers over Salahuddin and me. They also like to lift weights, so if duty calls, I think they could actually come to the rescue of their dear old Mom.

I walk out the back door, for the first time since Monday. The fresh air feels so good on my face. I carefully look around. No, there's no danger yet. I'm cautiously driving down the street, just a few blocks from home, when someone honks and yells something about going back home. That's happened before, and it always irritates because I want to tell the person that I am home. I start ranting.

"I am so tired of that. What's wrong with them? Do they have to stereotype everyone? That's been happening to me for twenty years now. Why won't they just stop it?"

"It's okay, Mom," says Muhammad. "That guy is just a jerk. It's no big deal."

"Yes, you're right, I guess. Well, let's see how things go at the store." When I walk into the grocery store, I cautiously look around at the other shoppers. Some of them are staring at me, I think. It's hard to tell, because when I look at them, they turn away. Anyway, that's not too surprising. No one says anything to my bodyguards and me. I carefully walk down the aisles, filling my cart with supplies for a hungry family, with my bodyguards at my side. Things are going well until I reach the cereal aisle. I'm checking for what's on sale, and not looking where I'm going, when I accidentally bump another woman with my cart.

"Oh, I'm sorry," I say, with greater emotion than the situation would usually warrant. "Please excuse me." Great, now there will be a report on the news tonight about the terrorist shopper.

The woman turns to look at me, and smiles. "It's okay," she says. "Don't worry about it." She turns back to her cart and walks away.

I was ready for a confrontation, and her polite response startles me. "Thank you," I mumble as I walk on up the aisle. After picking out some of the boys' favorite cereals, I continue on to the frozen foods. While filling the cart with tater tots and frozen onion rings, two of their favorite after-school snacks, I drop a bag. A man picks it up and hands it to me. "Here, let me help you."

I'm almost speechless. "Oh, uh, thank you," I stammer. These small kindnesses aren't at all what I'd expected. (It's also a good thing that man wasn't out to get me. My "bodyguards" are several feet away, picking out a couple half-gallons of ice cream.)

Finally, I finish filling the cart and go to the checkout line. While we stand in a long line, waiting for the cashier to do some price checks, the gray-haired woman behind me speaks up. "Excuse me for saying this, but you must have been frightened to come out today."

"Yes, I was. But people have been pretty nice."

"Most people are smart enough to know that it's certainly not your fault."

I smile. "Thank you for understanding." She smiles back.

Before heading back home, my bodyguards and I make a stop at Halal Choice, a Muslim store where I buy my meat, along with some other food and treats that are not sold in the general supermarket. I pick up eight fresh chickens and a ten-pound pack of ground beef, both of which I'll later divide into meals. I add three packages of lunchmeat, a box of chicken strips and two pizzas with beef sausage. Finally, I decide to throw in two packages of halal marshmallows, made without gelatin, for a special dessert.

I'm picking out my lunchmeat when Maryam walks in with Musa. It's so good to see her. We've talked on the phone a few times since that Tuesday morning, but it's been hard to carry on a conversation with the kids at home They're always interrupting to ask me something or tell on someone. Our hugs are especially tight today.

We've just finished giving our salaams when Khadijah walks in with her husband, Imran. They are both teachers at the Islamic school. Imran is a Palestinian and Khadijah is an American, like Maryam and me, but quite a bit younger. They don't have any children yet.

We all greet one another, and then get straight to the issue.

"So," I say, "what do you think all this is going to mean for us?"

"I don't know," Maryam responds, "but I can tell you one thing, girl. I've lived as a Muslim in this country for a long time. There are people who are against you no matter what, but most people aren't so bad. Anyway, I was black before I was Muslim, so I've already played that game."

"I know you have. I did notice that people were generally nice today."

"What I'm more afraid of," says Khadijah, "is the reaction of the other Muslims. I'll bet that some of these sisters are going to take their scarves off because they are so afraid."

I don't want to tell them about my own thirty-second struggle with that issue. Fortunately, I'm saved by the bell that rings when a new customer comes into the shop. It's an older Middle Eastern couple we all know. The woman, who has covered her head for as long as I've known her, is not wearing a scarf. She glances over at us shyly, without saying anything, then goes over to the canned goods. We also see that her husband has shaved off his long gray beard. We just look at each other and roll our eyes.

We talk quietly for a few minutes longer until our escorts, their husbands and my sons, impatiently remind us to move on. When I'm ready to pay for my purchases, I'm greeted by Ali, the owner and manager of the store.

"Assalaamu alaikum, Sr. Sadia. Do you think that it's safe for you to leave the house?"

I shake my head. "It looks bad, but this is my country, after all. Anyway, I have my two strong bodyguards with me." Muhammad and Sadeq each shake hands with Br. Ali. "Have you had any trouble with your business after the attacks?"

"Business has been a little slow these last few days, but I can understand that. My only real problem is that I'm going to have some trouble stocking fresh meat for a while."

"Why is that?"

"I've always gone to the same farmer to butcher the meat in the Islamic manner. Last Wednesday the farmer called and said that he doesn't want my business. I've been going to him for about four years now, but all of a sudden I guess he just doesn't trust me," remarks Ali in English tinged with an Arabic accent. He adds, "We're all going to have to be a little more careful now."

CHAPTER SIX

Under Attack

I'M ENJOYING THE fresh air and blue sky, the impersonal noise of the crowds, the acts of driving down the street and getting lost in my own thoughts. Now I have to think about going home.

We've been gone for about four hours. After buying the essentials, I decide to stop in a few more stores, just to browse. My favorite is the book store. I could have stayed until closing time, but my bodyguards are getting anxious.

"Mom," says Muhammad, "don't you think we should get back? Baba might get worried. Besides, Sadeq has to get ready for work."

There are many books I'd like to buy. I choose just one. A thick volume about conflicts in American history, it may help me to get some perspective.

Salahuddin is visibly relieved when we walk in through the back door. I'm carrying one bag of groceries, and about to go back for more, when he stops me.

"You can stay here. The boys and I will unload the car. Adam, Yusuf, I want you to come help."

He's acting strange. I shrug, and start putting things away.

When all of the groceries are unloaded and safely stored, Salahuddin comes up from behind and hugs me. "I was so worried about you," he whispers, his breath on my neck

I'm in the process of dividing up the ground beef for meals, but I turn around to face him. "Really, it was okay. People were actually nice. We didn't have any problem at

27

all." He looks worried. "What's wrong?"

"This afternoon a man was killed in Mesa, Arizona. He wasn't even a Muslim. He was Sikh. Someone was offended because he wore a turban, and shot him. Also, I didn't tell you what the imam told us about other attacks."

"What other attacks?"

"On Wednesday a mob held a demonstration in the streets of Bridgeview, Illinois, headed towards the masjid. They had to be stopped by the police. Gunshots were fired at a masjid in Irving, Texas, and bricks were thrown through the windows of an Islamic bookstore in Alexandria, Virginia. I didn't stop you from going out today, but I wanted to. You don't know how worried I was."

I give him a light hug. "Thank you for worrying. Alhamdulillah, we didn't have any trouble at all — except for some guy in a pickup truck who honked and told me to go home. That's happened so many times in the last twenty years that it almost feels normal."

"I want you to go out as little as possible. If you do go anywhere, you can't go alone for now. Either Muhammad or Sadeq will go with you, or I will. It's dangerous out there, Sadia. I just thank Allah that you didn't see that today."

I know he's right, but that doesn't mean I like it. I turn back to the ground beef and mutter, "Okay, I guess."

He kisses me on the cheek. "You know it's for your own safety. I just hope things get better soon." He walks away, probably to go check on the restaurant or watch television.

I left home for college when I was eighteen, and for four years I was on my own. I met Salahuddin in an accounting class in my sophomore year (when I was a business major). We got married two months after graduation, and six months after I accepted Islam. We moved a lot in the first years, until we decided to settle here. The town is small and friendly, and we thought it would be a good place to raise a family.

Then the kids started coming, and Salahuddin opened the restaurant, and I decided to stay home until the youngest started first grade. Two weeks after my youngest started first grade, the world fell apart, and now I'm sentenced to house arrest.

Many women blame their loss of freedom on getting married or having children. Marriage and children have slowed me down, but my biggest loss of freedom is coming from a terrorist attack that may have been perpetrated by men whose wives and mothers wear scarves, as I do.

Early Sunday morning, before the morning prayer at dawn, we are awakened by the phone. Salahuddin answers. It's someone from the alarm company, saying that there's a problem at the restaurant. The police have already been called.

"I have to go," he says when he hangs up. "They need me to be there when they check things out. I won't be gone long, insha Allah."

"Please be careful. Just stay out of the way and let the police do their jobs."

"Don't worry. Maybe the wind just triggered the alarm again."

It's still early, but I can't go back to sleep. I try to read, but can't concentrate. Time passes somehow, and Salahuddin has been gone for nearly an hour. I wake the boys up for the morning prayer. Normally, waking them up is not a task I enjoy. The only one who wakes easily is Amin. This time, though, I'm anxious for a little distraction.

"Where's Baba?" Muhammad asks when he comes downstairs for the prayer.

"The alarm company called. It was probably just the wind again. Hopefully, it's nothing."

"Hopefully," says Sadeq. He's probably imagining a scene from one of those action movies he watches too often. I know he has a vivid imagination, but it doesn't seem to bother him. My imagination usually makes me uneasy.

We pray, and Amin, Yusuf and Adam stay up to play while Muhammad and Sadeq go back to sleep. I wait anxiously for Salahuddin to come home. I think about calling the restaurant, but I don't want the police to think that I'm just another nervous, nagging wife (which I am).

The minutes pass, and Salahuddin has been gone for two hours. Finally, I decide to go ahead and call. I'm heading for the phone when it rings.

"Salahuddin?"

"Yes. I just wanted to let you know that I'll be home soon. The police need me to finish filling out some paperwork."

"Is everything okay? I guess it wasn't just the wind."

"No, there was some vandalism. I'll fill you in when I get home."

Relieved to hear from him, I doze until he comes home nearly an hour later. When he comes into the bedroom, the door squeaks. I roll over and groan.

"Salahuddin?"

"Yes, it's me."

I open my eyes and sit up, leaning against the oak headboard. "So, what was it?"

"Somebody threw a brick through the big front window. That's what triggered the alarm. They also painted graffiti on the side of the building, things like 'Go home, you dirty Moslems' and some profanity." He shakes his head. "I told you it's dangerous out there."

"What did the police say?"

"They'll keep up their patrols. They also said that I should close for a few days and hire a security guard. I'll need to hire someone to replace that window. I'll paint over the graffiti myself, and get Muhammad and Sadeq to help. I hope that the insurance covers this."

"I don't understand how this could happen. This has always been such a friendly town. That's why we decided to live here. We've been here for so many years, and the restaurant is part of the neighborhood."

"Things are changing. We will all have to be more careful."

"That's what Ali said yesterday. I can't believe that this is happening in my own country."

"Sadia, you have to stop living in the past. Times have changed. These are not the days when you were growing up and everyone talked about love and peace. It's rough now, and it's going to get rougher." His voice is getting tense.

"Okay. Why don't I make some breakfast, and then you can get some rest?"

"Thanks." He lies down on the bed. "Send one of the boys to get me when it's ready." I call Adam and Yusuf to help me in the kitchen.

After breakfast I take a short nap, while Adam and Yusuf clean up. Salahuddin rests a little more, too. When he gets up, he calls Sadeq and Muhammad.

"Let's go, boys. We're going to protest the cancellation of football games, remember? I've got some work for you at the restaurant."

Muhammad looks at Sadeq. "I told you he'd remember."

I do little things around the house, and the day passes quickly. When Salahuddin comes back with the boys, they're all splattered with white paint. Muhammad even has it in his hair.

They're quite a sight. "So, boys," I say in between laughs, "did you have fun?"

"Anyway, we got the job done," says Sadeq.

"You wouldn't believe all the junk they wrote," says Muhammad. "These guys are really ignorant. Man, I'd like to get my hands on them."

He's angry. I should be, too. But the sight of my three men covered in white specks has given me a rare comedic moment.

Salahuddin gets cleaned up, and soon it's time to go to the meeting at school.

"You don't have to go, Sadia. I can let you know what

was discussed."

"I'd really like to go. Besides, I'll be protected by the best bodyguard of all." I rub his back. He smiles.

CHAPTER SEVEN

Difference of Opinion

THE PARKING LOT is full. It's hard to find a place to park our van. Two of the fathers are already having a heated discussion outside the front door. This should be an interesting meeting.

I've been to many parents' meetings over the years. Usually not more than a handful even bother to show up. Everyone has busy lives and tons of excuses. This time, though, I think it's going to be different.

The principal calls everyone to order, and begins the meeting with a reading from the Qur'an. Then he starts, "As you all know, our school has received some threats since the attacks. This is why we decided to close the school this week. The purpose of the meeting tonight is to brief you on some of the ways we are working to make the school safer for your children."

He notes some of the steps that have already been taken, including the constant presence of a police car in the school parking lot, doors that will remain locked from the outside during the day and the cancellation of all field trips. The last point is disappointing to many parents, and I know the students won't like it. It will be hard for them to understand that this decision was made for their own safety

The principal continues, explaining that the teachers will receive special instruction from the police department on proper procedures during an emergency. Great. Along with fire drills and tornado drills, teachers now have to worry about drills on how to deal with Muslim haters and other terrorists. I hope they still have energy left for teaching.

The meeting is getting long. I hope the kids are okay.

"Finally," he says, "we need special help from the fathers. The times when we're most concerned about safety are in the mornings and afternoons, when the students are coming and going. We need some fathers to volunteer for patrol duty at these times. I'll pass around a sign-up sheet. Please indicate if you will be available in the morning or in the afternoon. This is a very important way for you to help in the security of our school. Are there any questions?"

Uthman is the first to raise his hand. He is a chemistry professor at the local university who has two daughters in the high school and a son, Fareed, in Adam's class. His wife, Asma, is a teacher at the school. He speaks in his thick Pakistani accent.

"I want to make sure that everyone is aware of the risks we are facing. My children will still come here, because I think it is a good school. But we should not try to fool ourselves. The Jews are out to defeat the Muslims in this land, and they will not stop until they succeed. I think —"

The principal interrupts. "Br. Uthman, we're not here to discuss politics. I'd like to ask everyone to refrain from making political statements. That's not the purpose of our meeting."

Uthman sits down, crosses his arms and hangs his head, chin against his chest. He doesn't look pleased, but he doesn't argue.

Imran, the social studies teacher, speaks next. "I don't agree with Uthman in his portrayal of the Jews, but I think I understand what he's trying to say. How many of you are aware that a Pakistani store owner was shot to death in Dallas last night? This is a very serious situation, and we need to do our best to protect the children."

The meeting continues on a practical note. There is some discussion about the exact safety measures to be taken, and fathers begin to volunteer for patrol duty. Salahuddin signs up for the afternoon shift. I'm sure he'd rather do mornings, but he's always having to wait for Adam.

After the meeting we stop to talk with Imran and Khadijah.

"I hadn't heard about the shooting of the brother in Texas, Imran," my husband says. "We really do have to be careful."

"Yes, we do have to be careful. But I don't want to hear anyone talk about 'the Jews' the way Uthman did just now. You know that I was born in Palestine. Many years before I was born, my family's land was stolen. I have cousins still living in Palestine who have to deal with checkpoints and harassment on a daily basis. It's a terrible situation. But if we start saying 'the Jews this' or 'the Jews that,' then we're no better than people who are saying 'the Muslims this' or 'the Muslims that.'"

I agree. "You're right. We can't let this just be about us versus them."

"Yes," adds Khadijah. "I think that's what terrorism is really all about."

While walking to our car, we're greeted by Hussein.

"I heard about the restaurant, Salahuddin. How bad is it?"

"It will be okay. I just need to make some repairs and hire a security guard. It could be worse. I keep thinking about the brother in Dallas."

"Yes. May Allah help his family. Personally, I think it might be better if we just pack up and take our families back home."

Salahuddin replies in a strong voice. "We came here for education and opportunities. My own wife and sons were born in this country. Am I supposed to uproot my family from their own home country just because of a few lunatics?"

Hussein counters, "This country isn't what it used to be, my brother. When we first came here, all you needed was a little hard work to make your way. But now, we are being branded the enemy without a judge or jury. Where is their liberty and justice? I'm sure that you understand this, Sr. Sadia."

"I certainly do, Br. Hussein. It's terrible that I have to feel like a stranger in my own country just because I pray five times a day and wear a scarf."

"But," Salahuddin interjects, "if you know anything about Americans, you'll know that she's very stubborn and not ready to give up without a fight." I give him a look.

Hussein laughs. "That's true, brother. But my wife is not an American, and she has already begun to pack. May Allah help you if you stay here."

"You're really leaving?"

"Yes, Sr. Sadia. I came tonight to see what it would be about, but I had already made up my mind. In my country, my children won't have to study behind locked doors, with a police car sitting out in front."

I hadn't even considered leaving, and didn't think that anyone else would, either. I have to admit, though, that I'm also disturbed by the necessity of putting my children's school under police protection. "What about Asiya? Does she want to go back?"

"It was her idea. She's been begging me all week to take them back home. She hasn't even left the house since the attacks."

"Well, I can understand that. I didn't get out until yesterday and, as Salahuddin says, it's my country. I'm really going to miss Asiya and the kids."

"Come to our house for dinner next week," says Salahuddin. "At least we can have a nice evening together before you leave."

"We'll come, if I can get Asiya to leave the house. I'll call you."

"May Allah help you in your decision," says Salahuddin.

"Amin," says Hussein. "May Allah hear your prayer and help us all."

CHAPTER EIGHT

Back to School

WHEN WE PULL into our driveway, we see that almost every light in the house is on. We walk into the living room to find all the boys sitting around the television, eating junk food and watching junk. Crumbs and toys are scattered on the floor.

"Assalaamu alaikum," Salahuddin booms. "Are you boys ready to go back to school tomorrow?"

"Um, no Baba." Adam jumps up and runs up the stairs to his room.

"Sorry about the mess," says Muhammad. "You know how the little kids are."

"Well, get it cleaned up," I say. "Then I want you all to make sure you have your uniforms and book bags ready."

"Do we have to go back?" asks Yusuf. "Maybe there will be some more attacks."

"You can't stay home forever. Now get ready."

"Why can't we stay home?" says Sadeq. "That sounds good to me."

"No more discussion. Get moving."

The next morning we fall right into our old patterns. Muhammad takes too long in the bathroom. Adam, who's had trouble sleeping since the attacks, is especially hard to wake up. Amin still doesn't want to tie his own shoes. It's frustrating, but at least it's normal.

The only one who doesn't act normal is Salahuddin. He has to sit in the car, waiting for Adam, for almost fifteen minutes, but he doesn't get upset. After you've witnessed a terrorist attack, I guess the little things are a lot easier to handle.

I kiss Salahuddin as he leaves the house. "Be careful when you're on duty this afternoon."

"I'm a experienced bodyguard, remember?" He winks and kisses me before going out to the car to wait for Adam.

Normally, on a Monday morning I would go to the library, go shopping or drop in on Maryam. Today, I can't do any of these. Salahuddin has been firm in not wanting me to leave the house without him, Muhammad or Sadeq, and frankly I agree. As much as I hate being a prisoner, I don't feel comfortable yet facing the world alone in my scarf.

Maryam can't come see me, either, because Musa feels the same way. So we have to be content with talking over the phone.

"How are your kids holding up over all of this, Maryam?"

"Ahmad's doing fine. His wife is a little nervous, but he always takes things in stride, just like his father. Ibrahim has to travel a lot with his job, so it's been tough for him. He was stranded in Seattle for three days last week. The boys are managing, though. I'm really worried about Laila. She just found out that she's pregnant, and now this. I'm trying to encourage her to be strong, but to tell you the truth, I wouldn't be too happy about bringing a baby into this world the way things are now. She already frets over little Yahya. That boy can't get a scrape, or even cough, without her fussing all over him. Now she has terrorism on her list of things to worry about."

"I know I'd have a hard time if I had real little ones these days. Like you said, you worry so much already. I'm glad that mine are at least half grown."

"Girl, I'm worried about my grown-up baby. I still hope Musa and I can go down there in a week or so."

We talk for about an hour, and then Maryam has to go. I walk through my quiet house, trying to decide what to do next. I don't like changes in my routine.

I piddle around for the rest of the morning. Finally, I decide to put my energy into a big dinner. I make wonton from scratch, cook up a big batch of chicken curry, and even decide to bake a chocolate cream pie for dessert. If this whole terrorism thing doesn't end pretty soon, I'll end up weighing three hundred pounds. By the time I'm able to leave the house freely, I won't be able to fit through the door.

Salahuddin brings the boys home a little late today, because of patrol duty after school. I don't know how long this will be necessary.

"Something smells good. You've been working hard," Salahuddin says, walking into the kitchen.

"I had to. I'm so bored just staying home. Anyway, how was patrol duty?"

"It was fine. Three other fathers showed up. Muhammad joined us, along with a few other senior boys. Nothing happened. It's hard to know what we should consider suspicious."

"Well, I think it's good that you're there, anyway."

He laughs. "I don't know who would be afraid of a short Asian man like me."

"Well, at least you have your big tall son to protect you, then."

Salahuddin stays home for a few minutes, then has to go to the restaurant for a couple of hours. The younger boys are playing, and the older boys are probably napping. Adam plays with his younger brothers for a while, then comes to hang around me in the kitchen as I put the finishing touches on dinner.

"Here, Adam, can you come chop these tomatoes for the salad?" I direct him to the cutting board on the counter. "How was school today?"

"It was okay. There was a police car sitting in the parking lot."

Salahuddin and I had decided not to tell the boys about

the police presence because we didn't want to alarm them. Now that I think of it, I probably should have told Adam ahead of time. Like me, he doesn't adjust easily to change.

"Well, yes, they're just there to help the school."

"Fareed said that people have been threatening to blow up the school."

"Oh, he's exaggerating. I'm sure that nothing like that will happen."

"Then why are the police there?"

I turn my attention away from the frying wonton to look at Adam. "Adam, we know that something very terrible happened last week. I don't think that anything else is going to happen." Well, maybe, but I don't want to pass my fears onto him. "But we have to be careful. I knew that the police were going to be there. I probably should have told you. They are just there to help us. Don't worry about it, okay?"

"Okay," he says, though he doesn't seem satisfied by my answer. He chops the rest of the tomatoes in silence. I become distracted, and almost burn the wonton.

During dinner the boys tell about their adventures of the first day back.

"I got a star for finishing my work and keeping my shoes tied," says Amin.

"Sr. Asma asked us what we did during the week," says Yusuf. "Most of the kids just complained because they couldn't watch cartoons. A lot of them have new video game systems, though. Can we get one, Mom?"

"I'll think about it," I say, taking the easy way out. We have an old system, without all the latest bells and whistles, but I'm not eager to invest in an upgrade. I don't like the idea of kids sitting for hours staring at a video game. It's hard to explain that to my boys, though, when almost all of their friends have the latest game systems. Our old, unsophisticated system is enough stimulation for them.

"Br. Imran wanted to talk about the attacks," says Sadeq. "Can you believe it? He said that he was scared. Man, I didn't think he was scared of nothing!" The bad grammar is for effect, of course. Imran is still fairly young himself, and he has a faithful following among the teen-age boys.

Muhammad has his own unique point of view, of course. "The funniest thing in our class was when Br. Imran asked Usama what he thought about the attacks. Usama said," Muhammad adopts a higher voice, complete with Arabic accent, "'You know how people like to make fun of me be-cause I'm fat. Try having a name like Usama these days!' The class just broke up. That Usama is one funny dude."

All of the boys start giggling, mostly because of Muhammad's rendition of the incident. Poor Usama, I think. "By the way, Sadeq, we almost named you Usama."

"I'm sure glad you didn't. I just hope there's no dude named Sadeq who starts blowing things up."

"Or Yusuf either," adds my ten-year-old. He continues, "Mom, the principal was talking in assembly about stereo-types. What's a stereotype?"

Before I can give a thoughtful answer, Muhammad barges in. "It's like saying that my brother Yusuf is a brat, so all Yusufs are brats."

"Muhammad!" He was so quiet as a child. It doesn't help that his brothers, including Yusuf, laugh at this and every other ridiculous remark.

I have to regain control. I wait a moment for them to settle down before beginning my lesson.

"A stereotype is when we judge a whole group of people by the actions of an individual who belongs to that group. So, for instance, when the news media says that nineteen Muslims hijacked the four planes, it would be a stereotype if someone said that all Muslims are dangerous people who might hijack planes."

Yusuf replies. "Can I say that all big brothers named

Muhammad are jokers?"

I give up. Class dismissed.

I'm starting to look forward to having a quiet house again tomorrow.

CHAPTER NINE

Guests for Dinner

SALAHUDDIN AND I decide to invite friends for dinner on Friday night. It will be a small going-away for Hussein and Asiya, who plan to leave in two weeks. We'll also invite Maryam and Musa, Khadijah and Imran and Asma and Uthman.

Planning for the dinner gives me something else to think about during my days of welcome silence and unwelcome isolation. I enjoy cooking, but I get tired of trying to make nice meals for my boys. The older ones eat as much as they can stuff into their mouths, without actually tasting the food. The younger ones always pick out the vegetables. All of them seem to prefer food from a can, box or drive-through over my home-cooked meals. I'm looking forward to cooking for people who will actually appreciate it.

Salahuddin takes me grocery shopping early Wednesday afternoon, before school is out. I don't need much, because I just went on Saturday and I like to stock up. Mostly, I want to get out among people again. I hope Salahuddin can see that there's no danger in the grocery store. A few people stare at us, but in all the trip is quite ordinary.

Salahuddin and I are very competitive in the kitchen. His older sisters taught him how to make curries, stir fry dishes and other Malaysian specialties. My mother taught me how to make spaghetti, pot roast and other American favorites. He is an excellent cook, and there have been times in our marriage, like after the births of our sons, when I was happy to let him take over. I refuse, however, to be overshadowed by my husband-chef. I make it clear to him that I will be in charge of this meal. I'll let him make the salad. Even his salad is excellent.

On Friday I scoot the boys off to school and take an hour or so to read before straightening up the house and starting on the dinner. I'll bake chicken, with my own secret recipe, and we'll have both scalloped potatoes and rice. I'll also have a shrimp appetizer and two cakes — one chocolate, all-American cake and one honey and almond Middle Eastern cake. At the last minute I decide to add a thin chicken soup to go with the rice. I don't know what kind of salad Salahuddin will be making. He said he wants to surprise me.

The menu reflects my experiences of the last twenty-five years. When I was growing up, I knew only people like me — white, Christian, middle class and at least third-generation American. In college I began to meet people from other areas of the world. It's been exciting to learn words from other languages and taste food from other lands. Most of the time this diversity adds an extra spice to life. Sometimes it's a challenge, though, to communicate effectively or even to eat together. My guest list includes friends from the Middle East, Pakistan and the United States, not to mention my Southeast Asian husband. My dinner will include potatoes and rice, American cake and Middle Eastern cake, as a sign of the struggle to know and get along with one another. My life has rarely been dull since that day when I first met a foreign student.

By the time the boys come home from school, everything is going smoothly. Salahuddin brings his salad that he prepared at the restaurant, and cautions me not to peek. It smells wonderful, but I'll wait.

I assign Muhammad and Sadeq to set up an eating area for the children. Hussein and Asiya have four children, two boys and two girls, all under the age of ten. Asma and Uthman have Fareed, two daughters in high school, and another two who are away at college. I'll put Asiya's children, Fareed and my three youngest at their own table. I'll need to expand our oak dining table to accommodate the teenagers so they can sit with the adults.

Muhammad and Sadeq want to eat with the adults, even though they think that most of us are old and boring. It's because they love to spend time with Musa and Imran. Imran is only about ten years older than Muhammad, and he has a good rapport with all the boys — playing basketball with them and talking about things they don't want to discuss with their parents (like school work, friends and pretty much life in general). Musa spent a lot of time working with youth during his years on the police force, and he still involves them in community service projects.

There are just a few more details to wrap up when Maryam and Musa arrive. They come early so Maryam can help me out. We haven't seen each other since last Saturday, and we hug tightly.

"So, how you doing, girl?" She grins. "Do you need me to rescue you?"

"Well, maybe just a little. What do you think of the soup?"

She tastes it. "Definitely needs more salt." She shakes some into the pot. "Musa and I decided to go see Laila next week. I think we'll be leaving on Sunday, insha Allah."

"That's great. I'm sure she'll be so happy to see you."

"You don't know the half of it. That girl has worked herself up into such a nervous state. I'm worried she could lose the baby if she doesn't find a way to calm down."

"Well, I'll keep praying for her. It's good that you're going. I'm sure she'll be okay."

"I made Musa take me out shopping today. I bought Laila some new maternity clothes, to pick up her spirit. And I spent, oh, a fortune on toys and clothes for Yahya. It's a good thing I don't have more grandchildren. We'd be broke." She stirs the soup and tastes it again. "Oh, this is much better. I don't know what you'd do without me."

Sometimes I don't know what I'd do without Maryam. We've been friends since I first moved to this town, when Muhammad was just a baby. She helped me learn the ins and outs of motherhood. Whenever I've needed help, she's been there, even while she was holding down a full-time job and raising teenagers. She retired last year from her job in the admissions office at the university. I'm glad she'll be able to be with Laila at a time like this.

We're just finishing up when Khadijah and Imran arrive. Adam, the doorman, leads Khadijah to the kitchen, while Imran goes to discuss current events with Salahuddin and Musa in the living room.

"Hi, ladies. How are you?" she greets us. We both greet her with warm hugs.

"We're fine. How's life in the outside world?" Maryam asks, as she goes to check on the cakes.

"You mean school? It's okay. The kids were a little nervous on Monday, and so was I. In our first 'anti-terrrorism' training session after school on Monday, the teachers were told that we may have to evacuate the building by having our students climb through the windows. The next day I kept trying to imagine how in the world I could get our big high school students through those small windows. Nothing happened, though, and by Friday I think things were almost back to normal."

"Were you able to talk to them about what happened?" I ask.

"We talked a little on Monday, but after that we had to get back to studying algebra. Imran has an easier time that way, as the social studies teacher. But he still has to stick to the syllabus. He says the kids want to keep talking about it. He thinks some of them are probably doing it to avoid getting homework."

"How is security at the school? Have there been any more threats?"

"I think there was one phone threat this week, but overall it's been quiet. The phones are tapped and, of course, we still have a police car sitting in the parking lot. The fathers have been good about keeping up the patrols in front. Of course, the kids were most upset about the cancellation of field trips."

"I bet," says Maryam. "I guess they're going to learn that life's not always fair."

"I guess so." Khadijah sighs as she says this. "Some psychologists say that it's good for children to experience some disappointment in their lives. Still, I hate to see the students be punished for something that wasn't their fault."

Maryam stops what she's doing and looks straight at Khadijah. I know what she's going to say. "Sister, when I was their age I couldn't drink at the same fountain as a white person, or go to the same school. Forget about field trips. It wasn't fair, and it wasn't our fault. Still, we had to pay the price. I'd rather not see it happen again to these kids, but sometimes that's the way life is."

Khadijah blushes. I know she's too young to remember the civil rights movement. She grew up as an American Muslim, with an American mother and a Turkish father. She's told me that her parents, both doctors, made sure that she had every opportunity.

Maryam notices Khadijah's embarrassment. "I'm sorry, honey. I didn't want to make you feel bad. Sometimes I forget that you're no older than Laila. When you get to be as old as me, though, you learn how to put things into perspective."

Khadijah smiles a little. "That's okay. I know I've lived a pretty sheltered life. I guess you're right. Imran's told me some stories about his childhood in Palestine, and I know that life is difficult for many people throughout the world." She sighs. "I just wish we could make the world perfect for the children."

Maryam and I both chuckle. We exchange looks, and she nods. I'll take this one. "I used to think the same thing, until I had kids. After you have children of your own, you'll find out that it's impossible to do anything perfectly. We all just do the best we can, and hope they turn out all right."

Everything's finished and I'm ready to serve the appetizers when Asma and Asiya arrive with their husbands. Asma is wearing a beautiful green Pakistani outfit, with wide-cut pants and a long tunic. Her scarf is tied in a special way that I've never been able to accomplish. I don't usually notice what other women wear, but I always notice Asma because she has excellent taste, and she always looks so "put together," especially for a mother of five.

I serve the appetizers, while we continue our small talk. We all pray the evening prayer together before eating dinner.

When Muslims get together for dinner, there are at least three possibilities when it comes to seating. Each couple can sit together. Or the women can sit at one end of the table while the men sit at the other end. Or the men and women can sit in completely separate rooms. Salahuddin and I prefer the second arrangement. There are general Islamic teachings about the separation of men and women, but many of the details are cultural.

When we gather around the table, I sit next to Salahuddin at one end, and Maryam sits next to Musa at the other end. The other wives and Asma's two teenage girls sit between Maryam and me. The other husbands and my two teenage boys sit between Salahuddin and Musa.

I've gone to many parties where the women sit in a separate room. On those occasions the conversation generally revolves around children, cooking, clothes and cosmetics. On the way home I compare notes with Salahuddin and learn that the men were discussing world politics. I'd rather sit with the men.

At first the conversation is segregated. Asma compliments me on the soup, and Maryam grins. I don't know what the men are talking about. The mood is subdued as we enjoy the food. Salahuddin leans over and whispers, "Good job." I bask in the praise from the master chef.

Imran is the one who breaks the ice. "So, Br. Hussein, what is it that made you decide to return to your country?"

"I'll tell you, Imran. I love this country. When I first came, back in '85, I had no complaints. After a few years I married Asiya and brought her over, and all of our children were born here. People are usually nice, and the opportunities are good. Things started to get tough around the time of the Gulf War, but it wasn't too bad. In the last two weeks that has all changed. You all know about the threats — to the school, to all of us. My wife doesn't want to leave the house, and my children keep crying because they are so afraid. Last night the president said that either you're with us or you're with the terrorists. He doesn't understand that most of us are just trying to survive."

"Yes," Uthman agrees. "It's getting very bad."

Hussein continues. "Back in my country I still have the freedom to live my life and support my family. My wife can go to the market without fear. If I thought it would get better, I'd stay. But, my brother, I'm afraid that it will only get worse."

"But, Br. Hussein," Imran protests, "I think you're making a rush to judgment. This is still a fine country. I think that if we just hold together and stay strong, we'll be all right in the end. The American people are still suffering from the shock of the attacks. We just need to be patient. I think things will turn around."

"You're too young, Imran. You don't know what you're talking about," says Uthman. "Do you think this problem has just started? No, it's been going on for years. They've been trying to get rid of Islam for a long time now, and this attack is their greatest victory. Kill innocent people and blame it on the Muslims. They're plotting against us, Imran, and they won't be satisfied until they wipe us out!" Uthman pounds the table with his fist. The table shakes and the dishes rattle.

Everyone is silent. Even the smaller children stop their

playful chatter.

Imran stands his ground. "I'm sorry, Br. Uthman, but I don't agree with you. I know who you mean by 'they,' and I feel it's wrong to stereotype any group of people in that manner. More importantly, I feel that it's detrimental to assume that there is an organized effort against Islam." His voice is strong and unwavering, but he is beginning to perspire.

Right now I wish I was sitting in a room with only women, talking about diaper rash and dried-on stains.

Uthman rises from his chair, shouting. "You don't know anything. I don't know why they even let you teach at that school. None of us is safe. You will see. They are out to get us all!" I'm afraid he'll keep on yelling and blustering, but Musa stands up and grabs Uthman by the shoulder.

"Uthman, get hold of yourself. Come with me."

Uthman looks at Musa, glares back at Imran and then follows Musa into the living room. It's easy for him to get angry at Imran, a young man with fresh ideas. But Uthman has known Musa for over twenty years. When they first met, Uthman was the young man with fresh ideas. He even stayed with Maryam and Musa a few times when he was still a student and the dorms were closed for vacations. Now, Uthman is again the young man who obediently, though reluctantly, follows his mentor.

There's an awkward silence at the table. Sadeq looks stricken at hearing his favorite teacher rebuked. Imran is quietly fuming, in his own controlled manner. Hussein, who probably feels somewhat responsible for the fuss, pushes his rice around the plate. We wives wait anxiously.

I don't know what to say. My beautiful evening has been ruined. I sit and stare at my plate. I begin to study the miniature shrimp and papaya in Salahuddin's very delicious salad.

Salahuddin must have noticed my gaze. My hero is the one who breaks the tension when he says, with flourish,

"Sadia, you haven't said anything yet about my wonderful salad. Do you want me to give you the recipe?"

I laugh, in spite of myself, and everyone else begins to laugh. We breathe a collective sigh of relief, and cautiously return to eating and small talk.

Musa and Uthman return about ten minutes later. Uthman walks over to Imran and offers his hand.

"I'm sorry, Imran. You're a good teacher and a fine young man. I don't always agree with you, but you are a good man."

Imran stands and accepts Uthman's outreached hand. The two men even hug and slap each other fondly on the back. (Muslims hug each other a lot.)

The rest of the evening goes smoothly, with no more mention of politics. The other women help me clear the table, and offer to wash the dishes as well. I politely decline, even as they persist. Salahuddin has promised to wash the dishes after our company leaves and, although I'm no longer the feminist I was in college, I enjoy seeing men do housework.

Asma is amazed. "Your husband washes dishes? Uthman does the yard work, but I've never been able to get him in the kitchen."

"Not Hussein, either," says Aliya. "In our country the women have to do all the work around the house. That's how we are raised."

The evening ends as it began, with the women in the kitchen and the men in the living room. When I first became a Muslim, I hated the idea of separation by gender. I've come to notice, though, that sometimes it's very natural. I can recall holidays at my grandmother's house when the women gathered in the kitchen, cooking and gossiping, and the men sat in the living room, watching football and napping.

The time soon comes for our guests to leave. We escort each couple to the door and say our goodbyes. Before Uthman leaves, he apologizes to me.

"I'm sorry, Sr. Sadia, for disrupting the dinner. I worry

so much these days."

"That's okay." Yes, I think, we're all worried.

When all the guests are gone, Salahuddin squeezes my shoulder and kisses me on the cheek. "Nice dinner. You really are a good cook."

"Well, thank you very much, sir."

"So, do you want the recipe for my salad?"

I chuckle as Salahuddin leads Muhammad, Sadeq and Adam into the kitchen to help him with the dishes.

Let the men do the work. I'm going to bed. Suddenly, I'm exhausted. The dinner's over and I'm ready for a good night's sleep.

CHAPTER TEN

Detention

I REST MY head on the pillow and feel myself falling. The sensation is pleasant, like tumbling into a pile of snow as a child. I don't know how much time passes, but gradually the pleasant feeling is replaced by something more ominous. I have to get up, but I can't. My body is weighed down. I hear Amin crying for me. He sounds so far away. I have to go help him, but I can't get up.

The phone rings. I sit straight up in bed, relieved to be finally free of the unseen bonds. I listen for Amin's cries, but the house is quiet except for the persistent ringing of the phone. Breathing deeply, I try to make sense of the experience. Only vaguely do I hear Salahuddin grumble, "Never mind, I'll get it."

His complaint wakes me from my daze. Amin is safely asleep in his bed. I'm sure of that now. I can move. There was nothing holding me. It was just a dream.

I try to focus on the source of my liberation. The phone. What's happening? It must be the alarm company. "Not again," I moan sleepily as I lie back down.

"What happened?" I hear him say. "Who came? Why did they do that? Okay, we'll be right there."

We. Did he say we?

"Sadia," he whispers, shaking me gently. "Sadia, wake up. That was Asma's daughter."

Asma's daughter? Does she work for the alarm company?

"Sadia, wake up. Asma needs our help."

I groan again, and look at the clock through half-open

eyes. It's 2 a.m. It's 2:01 by the time I can actually speak.

"What is it," I yawn. "What happened?"

"They've arrested Uthman."

Now I'm awake. "They what?"

"Asma's daughter called and said that they've arrested Uthman."

I jump out of bed, slip into one of my dresses, pin on my scarf and head for the door. By the time I get there, Salahuddin is already in the car waiting for me. I don't know how he does that.

The streets are dark and peaceful. It would be easy to believe that there is no trouble underneath the thin crescent moon.

We ring the doorbell. Fatima, Asma's older teenage daughter, lets us in. Another daughter, Hakima, is sitting next to Asma on the couch, trying to comfort her. Fareed sulks in a corner.

My chest constricts as tears come to my eyes. I go to Asma, and Salahuddin approaches Fareed.

"Assalaamu alaikum, Fareed." He puts his right arm around Fareed's shoulders, and Fareed responds by holding on to Salahuddin and crying softly.

I sit on the couch, along with Hakima, trying to soothe Asma. We've been like this for several minutes when Maryam and Musa arrive. Maryam comes over and strokes Asma's head, as if she were a child

The only sound in the room is Asma, quietly sobbing. Then, suddenly, Fareed shouts out, "They're liars. My dad's not a terrorist!"

Fareed's outburst causes Asma to cry even harder.

"Let's go, Fareed. Why don't we go to your room, and we can talk," says Salahuddin.

"My dad is not a terrorist!"

"Let's go, son," says Musa.

Between the two of them, Musa and Salahuddin get Fareed to come with them. As he walks, he keeps shouting,

"He's not a terrorist." Each time it pierces my heart. I can only imagine how Asma feels.

The shouting fades as the men take Fareed up the stairs and into his room. Finally, it is silent again.

We women sit together, helplessly sharing Asma's grief and anxiety. We talk to her quietly, we hug her and we wait.

Hours seem to pass before Asma is composed enough to talk. Her eyes are red and her face is swollen. Fatima brings her some water, which she drinks reluctantly but gratefully in small sips.

"They came to the door about fifteen minutes after we got home." Asma begins her narrative slowly, in a voice on the verge of tears. "Later, I thought about it. I think they were probably parked outside, waiting for us to come home. So they came to the door and identified themselves as government agents. They said they wanted to ask Uthman some questions. I could tell that Uthman was worried, but I guess he hoped that if he cooperated they would just go away.

"At first, Uthman was calm. You remember when Musa talked to him? That seemed to help because he was very calm. He was under control. But then they kept on asking questions, and they wouldn't go away. They just kept on asking. Uthman started to get agitated again. He became angry, and he started saying things. You know how he is. So they kept on asking and he kept on getting angrier. I couldn't get him to calm down. If I could just have made him calm down."

"It's not your fault," I say. "What happened then?"

"You know how Uthman is. He started talking about the World Trade Center attacks, blaming the Jews and the government. He began screaming all these strange accusations. The next thing I knew, they had him in handcuffs. Then, he got real quiet." Tears roll down Asma's cheeks. "Then he knew. But it was too late."

"What did they say?" asks Maryam. "Did they tell you

why he was being arrested?"

"They just said that he's on a list of suspected terrorists. Can you imagine? Just because he talks too much and gets angry sometimes? They said that they needed to take him in for more questioning."

"Did they tell him what evidence they have, or what the charges are? Did they ask him if he wanted to contact an attorney?"

"No. They just took him away in handcuffs."

I don't believe what I'm hearing. "They can't do that."

Maryam shakes her head. "How many times do I have to keep telling you, girl. They can and they will. This isn't new."

"No," I sigh, "I guess it isn't."

"You saw Fareed. I just hate what this is doing to my kids." She strokes Fatima's hair and squeezes Hakima's hand. "It's not right to take their father away from them."

We stay with Asma and her family for more than three hours. About an hour before sunrise we pray the morning prayer together, and then we have to head home to get our own boys up to pray.

Musa says he will try to use his ties with law enforcement to help Uthman. He admits, though, that his efforts may be fruitless. "I was with the local force," he explains. "You're talking about the feds. That's a whole other scene."

We leave Asma, encouraging her to try to get some sleep. As I walk out the front door, she begins to cry again. "What will I do, Sadia?"

I hate to admit that I just don't know.

CHAPTER ELEVEN

Facing Facts

UTHMAN HAS BEEN arrested. I sit silently in the car
on the way home, trying to digest this fact. What will it
mean for Asma and her family? What will it mean for the
rest of us?

Salahuddin and I struggle home, make sure the boys
have made their morning prayers, and go to bed. We leave
Adam in charge of watching his younger brothers, while
Muhammad is supposed to make breakfast for them all
and Sadeq will (I hope) clean up. Then we go to get a few
hours of sleep. I hope that Asma will be able to sleep.

Sleep comes quickly, but not peacefully. I have persistent visions of strange men. Some are knocking at doors.
Others are hiding — hiding in cars, behind bushes, in my
backyard. I toss and turn, trying to make the strange men
go away.

Finally the strange men do go away and I open my eyes.
Sunlight is streaming through the large window on the
other side of the room. It must be noon.

When I step out into the hall, I'm amazed that the house
is still in one piece, and quiet, too. The younger boys are
playing in their room. Their door is open.

"Assalaamu alaikum, guys."

"Boy, Mom, you really slept late," says Yusuf. "What
happened?"

Should I tell them? Eventually I'll have to say something. Adam is sure to find out from Fareed, and Asma is
Yusuf's teacher. Let me have my coffee first.

"I guess I was just really tired."

"Oh, okay." He goes back to playing with his action figures.

I go downstairs to find a kitchen that's almost spotless. There are portions of leftover scrambled eggs stored neatly in the refrigerator. It's nice to know the boys can manage on their own if they need to.

I put on a pot of coffee and stick a bagel in the toaster. I'll probably need at least two cups to get started today.

I hear voices from the television in the living room. Muhammad's watching football. It is late. Sadeq is probably in his room, getting ready for work.

I've been thinking about Muhammad's future a lot lately. He's in his senior year and plans to major in computer science. The state university he wants to attend is about 200 miles away. This might be a good time to talk to him. I finish my breakfast and go sit next to him on the couch. His favorite quarterback is going for a touchdown. I'd better wait until the next commercial.

When the commercial comes on, he's in a good mood, quietly celebrating the touchdown. It seems like a good time.

"You know, Muhammad, times are pretty rough right now. There are attacks on Muslims in different cities, and even some arrests. Br. Uthman was arrested last night. Baba and I went over there when Fatima called to tell us. That's why we're so tired."

He looks away from the beer commercial — which, unfortunately, is quite entertaining. "Br. Uthman was arrested? Why?"

"Sr. Asma said that government agents came to talk to him, and after some questioning they just took him away."

"I bet he got angry, just like he did here at our house."

"Yes, I'm sure he did. I don't know if that made any difference or not."

"Did they say why they arrested him?"

"Only that he is suspected of links to terrorism."

"Cool!"

"Muhammad!"

"I'm sorry, Mom. It's just that I've never known anyone who was arrested before, especially not a terrorist."

"Br. Uthman's not a terrorist."

"I know. I mean, he probably isn't."

The game's back on. "Anyway, Muhammad, this thing is affecting all of us."

Reluctantly, he glances away from the screen. "Yeah, I guess."

"Your father may have more trouble at the restaurant, and I can't even think about applying for a job right now. The government is talking about war — war on terror, maybe even war in Afghanistan. They say it isn't against Muslims, but you know how people can get it all turned around."

"Yeah, I know." He pretends to be listening, while directing most of his attention to the action on the field.

"So, Muhammad, I've been thinking. What if you just go to the community college or the local university next fall? You could live at home, which would save money. It might also be safer. Right now I'd be so worried if you were on your own somewhere. What do you think?"

The receiver from the opposing team is running down the field with the ball, but Muhammad turns around and looks at me. It will be hard to forget that look on his face. I know that he's been waiting to get away and be on his own. I remember that feeling. If my mother had told me I shouldn't go away to college, I probably would have gotten into a big argument with her. Fortunately, my sons learned at an early age that it isn't wise to talk back, so Muhammad doesn't say much. He just looks down, says, "Whatever you think," and goes upstairs to his room. His only protest is the unnecessary force he uses to shut his door. He'll probably go to his computer to try to forget the troubles of the world.

I hate to discourage his dreams. I really do remember

how it felt to be eighteen and wanting to get out on my own. But times are so tough, and even though he's six feet tall, he's still my first baby. I just don't think I can let him go right now. I'm sure my mother wouldn't have let me go if things had been this bad. I'll talk with Salahuddin about it, and maybe later the three of us can sit down together for a real conversation. He always listens to his father.

During that first week, when the boys acted as if they didn't care about the attacks, I knew that they really did care. They just needed time to figure out how the attacks are going to affect them personally, beyond the rescheduling of football games. They could be facing changes in college plans, and a possible draft. The time has come for the two of them to face facts.

I'm lost in thought when Muhammad and Sadeq come down the stairs. "Mom," says Sadeq, "Muhammad's going to drive me to work."

"I need to go to work a few hours today, too," says Muhammad. "I'll pick up Sadeq when he's done." He heads for the front door, then turns around. "I'll think about what you said, Mom."

That's all I need. At least he's listening.

Both boys have outside jobs. When they were younger, from about ages ten to sixteen, they helped Salahuddin at the restaurant. When each boy turned sixteen, it was Salahuddin who encouraged him to get a job. He wants each of them to work for a boss who isn't a relative, someone who will hold them accountable. Muhammad works a few evenings a week and some weekend hours at a computer store. Sadeq works on the weekends at the local branch of a national pharmacy.

When the boys come home from work, we're just finishing dinner. They're both laughing. "What's so funny?" asks Yusuf.

"Let me tell it," says Muhammad.

"No, it's my story," says Sadeq.

"So, what was it?" I ask.

"Okay, there was this one customer, an old man. I'm stocking shelves when he and his wife come up to me. The old man says, 'Son, can you show me where to find the denture adhesive?'

"I tell him it's in the middle of aisle six. He's about to go when he turns around and looks at me strangely. He's reading my name tag. 'Saadik. That's a strange name. Are you one of those Moslems?'" As he tells the story, Sadeq emphasizes the "o" on "Moslems."

He continues. "I tell the man, yes, I am a Muslim. He says something like, 'You better just tell your people to leave this country alone. If they don't like it here, they can just go live in their tents.' Can you believe it?"

Yusuf laughs loudly. "I know. People in Singapore don't even have tents."

"What did you do?" I ask. I hope he wasn't disrespectful to the misguided old man.

"Oh, I just said, 'Yes, sir', and went back to stocking the shelf. But I heard him talking to his wife as they walked off. He says, 'It's those foreigners who cause so much trouble in this country. Maybe we should just ship them all back.' He's so ignorant. He doesn't even know that I was born here. Whatever. He was weird."

"At least you handled it well. I'm proud of you for that."

"Yeah, sure. What could I do anyway?"

"Okay, now let me tell it," says Muhammad.

"Were you there, too?" asks Adam.

"No, but I know about people like him. I see them all the time."

Muhammad's rendition has the whole family laughing. He embellishes on the old man, imitating his walk and adding a few more choice statements about terrorists.

I never allow the boys to be disrespectful to the elderly. Still, I'm reluctant to stop Muhammad's farce. These boys have spent most of their lives hearing that Muslims are terrorists. Being able to laugh at the situation, if only for a moment, just seems to make it more bearable. Sometimes the easiest way to get through life is to look for the joke.

CHAPTER TWELVE

A Little Encouragement

MARYAM AND I visit Asma again on Sunday afternoon. Salahuddin and Musa come with us, of course, and we bring the younger boys. Salahuddin and Musa will take Fareed and the boys out for a while, probably to the park with a stop for burgers. It should help Fareed to get out a little.

Maryam and Musa have decided to postpone their trip for a couple more days, to see if they can help Asma and Uthman. I know Maryam is worried about Laila, but she doesn't want to abandon Asma. They're still hoping to leave for Texas by midweek.

Fatima answers the door. When we walk in, Asma greets us as if everything is normal. She doesn't look good, though. There are dark circles under her eyes, and her face looks older somehow. Instead of her usual fashions, she's wearing an old gray bathrobe. It probably belongs to Uthman.

The news isn't good. Asma still doesn't know where her husband is. Musa and the imam of our community have tried to get some information, but they've also come up empty-handed. All any of us knows is that he's being held in an undisclosed location and formal charges haven't been brought against him yet.

Asma is calmer than she was early Saturday morning, but she exudes a quiet distress. Throughout the visit she wrings her hands nervously, as if the mere motion will somehow ensure her husband's safe return.

"I called Aliya and Farhia. They'll be coming home."

Aliya and Farhia are her older twin daughters. They're studying pre-med and journalism, respectively, at the university Muhammad wants to attend.

"What about their studies?" I ask.

"Hopefully they'll be able to transfer to the university here. Uthman wanted them to go there, anyway, but they wanted to be on their own — and he always had such a hard time saying no to them. You know how it is."

Yes, I know.

"I guess I'll have to call the university to let them know what's happened. Uthman's been there for almost twenty years. They should understand."

"I'll call them for you," Maryam offers.

"Oh, thank you, that would help. I don't know what I'll do. I've got to keep teaching, but I haven't been able to even think about lesson plans. Fatima and Hakima help around the house. I can't seem to do anything. I still can't believe they took him. He can be loud and opinionated, but he's no terrorist."

Neither Maryam nor I know what to say to comfort Asma. We just sit with her for the next two hours, until our bodyguards return. It was little comfort later when we learned that hundreds of men were arrested during the first two weeks after the attacks. That just means that hundreds of families are waiting.

* * * * *

The weekend has been so rough, and I'm not really looking forward to the coming week. On Monday morning, after the boys leave, I just lie around the house, unable to focus. I can see the work that needs to be done, but I just feel too overwhelmed to do it. By 1:00 I finally manage to clean up the kitchen, and dinner is in the oven soon after the boys come home. Otherwise, my day is wasted. I'm too tired to do anything, and too anxious to rest.

When the boys come home, they're noisy and energetic, as usual. They grab some snacks and go rest or watch cartoons before dinner and homework.

Adam hangs around me in the kitchen. I think he wants to talk.

"How was school, today, Adam?"

"It was okay. Fareed was real quiet. He didn't even want to play basketball, and he's the best in the class. Do you know when his dad will get to come home?"

"No, I don't. I wish I did."

"Something else happened, too. It was something good, though. Some people came to our school from the Catholic school down the street, and they brought a big banner with them. The kids in their school had drawn pictures on it and wrote things like 'We'll pray for you' and 'We're your friends.' The principal had a special assembly after dhuhr. The people from the Catholic school gave us the banner and said some nice things about our school. They even said stuff about how they know it wasn't our fault."

I'm often guilty of listening to my kids with half an ear, while I do or think about something else. But Adam has my full attention this time.

"They did that for our school?"

"Yeah, it was cool. They even told us we shouldn't worry because we have lots of friends like them. They said they know that most Muslims aren't bad."

"That's great, Adam. I'm really glad that they did that."

"Me, too." He walks off down the hall, eating a banana.

All day I've been carrying an invisible weight on my shoulders. When I had to stop leaving the house without a bodyguard, I felt oppressed. When Uthman was arrested — granted, he has radical opinions and a big mouth, but I really don't think he's a terrorist — the weight of oppression became heavier.

When I thought about Muhammad having to change his college plans and Sadeq being confronted with ignorance at his work, the weight became heavier still.

When I thought about Asma trying to cope without her

husband, the burden was almost unbearable. Now, when Adam tells me about a few kind words from strangers, the oppressive weight lightens a little. It's still there, but I don't feel immobilized by it as I was earlier today.

We eat a quiet dinner. I think we're all feeling it, that invisible burden. Even Amin is quieter, paying attention to his rice and chicken without his typical little songs.

Dinner is finished and the table has been cleared when the phone rings. It's probably Maryam or Asma, or maybe Khadijah. I answer, "Assalaamu alaikum."

"Hello, Mrs. Abdullah. I don't know if you remember me. This is Jean. I used to work at the library."

Yes, Jean. I remember her. I went to her retirement party about six months ago.

"Yes, Jean, how are you? How's your retirement?" I wonder why she's calling me. She doesn't have to worry about my overdue books any more.

"Oh, I'm fine. I've been keeping busy, doing lots of traveling. The reason I called is that I've been worried about you. I've heard that the Muslim community has been having some trouble."

I'm caught off guard by her comment. "Oh, well, yes, I guess there's been some trouble."

"I've been reading about problems Muslims are experiencing in other cities. Have you had many problems here?"

I don't want to talk about the vandalism at Salahuddin's restaurant and Uthman's arrest, or even about my bodyguards. "We're getting along okay, I guess. Things have changed, though."

"Yes, I know. That's why I called. I just wanted to let you know that I'm thinking about you all, and praying for you."

I'm stunned by her concern. "Well, thank you. That really means a lot."

"Most people aren't against Muslims. You have a lot of

support in the community. Unfortunately, there are some people who make things difficult for all of us."

"Yes, there are." I am thinking about Salahuddin's restaurant and the attacks in the other communities that made my husband convinced I need bodyguards.

"Well, I just wanted to call you to let you know that you have some friends in the community. There really are a lot of people who care. I hope you remember that."

"Yes, I will. Thank you so much for calling."

"Goodbye, Mrs. Abdullah. I hope to talk to you later."

"Yes, I hope so. Again, thanks so much for calling. Goodbye."

I hang up the phone, and the weight becomes lighter. Jean is a special lady. She read stories to the children on Saturday mornings, and no matter how tall my boys have grown, she always remembers their names. I will never forget her kindness.

As the week passes, I find more reasons to have hope, and the weight continues to lighten. Each day when my boys come home they tell me about more acts of kindness towards the school. There are cards, letters and more banners. Students from across the city are showing their support for the Muslim students in our little school. Church leaders are also coming forward. One church sent a beautiful bouquet of flowers to our school.

Our high school students form an ad hoc committee to respond to these kindnesses. Muhammad is recruited to join. They write thank you letters and plan joint activities with students in the other schools. On Wednesday Muhammad tells us that the girls in our school will be working with the girls in the Catholic school to send stuffed animals to children in New York City. Amin decides to give one of his favorite stuffed bears to the project.

The weight of oppression eases, ever so slightly, with every act of kindness. It is still there. Just knowing that other people care, though, makes it so much easier.

Salahuddin has been tense all week, too. The restaurant re-opened last Thursday, with a new picture window and no trace of graffiti. A guard comes on duty in the evening and watches the place all night. But business has been slow. I guess word of the vandalism spread, and people don't feel comfortable coming back. Most evenings Salahuddin just goes to sit on the couch, watching the news.

On Wednesday evening, after the kids have gone up to their rooms, I sit next to him. "What's wrong? You've been so quiet lately."

"Business is bad, Sadia. I don't want to talk about it."

I go upstairs, leaving him alone. He doesn't come to bed for several hours.

On Thursday afternoon when the kids come home, I'm sitting in the living room, reading. Lately Salahuddin has just dropped the boys off and headed back for the restaurant. This time, though, he walks in, comes over to the couch and leans over me. He nuzzles my cheek and neck.

"You smell good." His beard tickles.

I pull back, surprised. "What happened to that grouchy man who's been living here all week?"

He stops nuzzling and looks at me. He's grinning.

"You won't believe what happened today. Business has been so slow, I wondered if we'd ever get back to normal. I was even worried that we might have to close."

I didn't know it was that bad.

"Today was the same. It was time for lunch, but we only had two customers — Brett, from the bookstore down the street, and Saleh, who bought Hussein's place. I was about to tell some of the workers to go on home, and then it happened. They started coming in. There were at least twenty of them. Reverend Wilson, from the Methodist church, was leading. He came up to me and said, 'I'm sorry it took us so long to get over here. We want you to know that we support your business, and I personally hope you don't even think about closing. I'm real hungry for some of that chicken curry right now.' Then they all sat down and had lunch. I need to get back soon, because Reverend Wilson said he's bringing in some more people for dinner." Salahuddin tells his story with excitement. "You were right, Sadia. The restaurant is part of the neighborhood."

The weight eases. "I'm so glad I was right. I was starting to wonder, too. At least, it's good to know that the 'war on terror' hasn't changed our neighbors."

He kisses me. "Thank you for supporting me."

Amin is calling from the top of the stairs. "Mom, can you come here?"

"I've got to get back, anyway," he says. "I might be late."

"I'll wait up."

He kisses me again and walks out the back door, the triumphant warrior heading back into battle.

* * * * *

During dinner Yusuf says, "We saw a really good movie in school today. We got to watch a movie yesterday, too."

I'm puzzled. "What kind of movies are they?"

"You know, regular movies. Like the kind they have in the theater."

I'm starting to get concerned. "Why are you watching movies in class? Do they teach you something about social studies or science?"

"No, they're just fun."

"Did Sr. Asma say why your class is watching the movies?"

"No, she didn't really say anything. She just cries a lot."

I've been trying to keep in touch with Asma, but it's hard getting over to visit during the week. I called on Wednesday and talked with Aliya, who had just gotten back in town. No one knows yet where Uthman is, or what the charges are against him.

I'm not really surprised when Yusuf comes home on Friday with some news. "Mom, Sr. Asma said that she's not going to teach us any more. She said we're going to have a new teacher. Do you know why she can't teach us? I'm really going to miss her." He pauses a moment. "Who will our new teacher be?"

I haven't talked with Yusuf about Uthman's arrest, though I'm sure he's heard some gossip around school. "I don't know" is all I can say.

Muhammad is upset by the news. "Man, Sr. Asma is a good teacher. I remember when she helped me do a project about Native Americans. And she's the one who first taught me about computers."

"And she brought a treat for us every Friday," Sadeq adds.

"She didn't yell at us, either, not even when we were bad," says Adam.

And so a qualified and well-loved teacher becomes an indirect casualty of the September 11 attacks and the resulting war on terror. I suspect that it's the students who will suffer the most

I think about Asma as I clean up the kitchen and wash the dishes. I'm just about to settle down for some TV when the phone rings. It's the principal.

"Assalaamu alaikum, Sr. Sadia. I wonder if you could help us out."

"What is it?"

"You know that Sr. Asma has been very upset over her husband's detention. She came to me today and said that she's decided to quit teaching, at least until her husband returns. I'm afraid that could take several months."

"Yes, she's been having a very hard time."

"So you know then that we have a problem. I need more time to find a qualified teacher to replace Sr. Asma. Right now I don't have anybody."

"What are you going to do?"

"That's why I'm calling. I was wondering if you'd be willing to take over Yusuf's class for a few days until we can find another teacher."

No, no, no, I say to myself. There is no way that I can

spend the whole day in a classroom with a bunch of Yusufs. One of them is plenty, thank you. I decided in college that I could never be a teacher. No, thank you, I would rather just go to the dentist every day next week.

"Well, I guess, if it's just for a few days, yes, I could help out."

"Thank you, Sr. Sadia. I'll make sure that the materials are ready for you on Monday morning. I really appreciate your help."

I really wish I could keep my mouth shut.

CHAPTER THIRTEEN

School Days

WHAT HAVE I gotten myself into?

I wish I could talk to Maryam about it, but they finally left for Texas yesterday. They're not sure how long they'll be gone. "As long as my baby needs me," is what she said.

When I tell Salahuddin about the conversation, including my inner voice, he laughs. "It will be a good experience," he says.

"So was childbirth."

"How bad can it be?"

I don't know, but I guess I'll find out.

On Monday morning I put on a plain blue dress and climb into the van with the boys to go to school. How bad can it be? They're only kids. Then again, so were the Nazi youth.

When I told the boys the news, Yusuf laughed even louder than his father had. "You're going to be my teacher? But you're not a teacher, Mom."

Well, no, kid, I guess I'm not. But I did teach you how to walk and talk and a million other things. Maybe I can be a teacher.

In a classroom all day with twenty other Yusufs? Maybe not. We'll see.

The principal meets me at the school door.

"I'm so happy you could help us, Sr. Sadia. This should only be for a few days, until we can find someone to take Sr. Asma's place." He walks with me to the classroom and briefly goes through the schedule and learning materials on the desk. "You'll be fine. Just let me know if you need anything."

I sit at the desk, trying to acquaint myself with the materials while the students are still in assembly. There's so much information — the daily schedule, classroom rules, student roster and attendance sheet and, of course, the lessons themselves. I've barely settled in when I hear a loud noise in the hallway. It's the sound of twenty-one fifth graders heading my way, and there's no time to take cover. Ready or not, here they come.

I've known most of these kids since they were babies, or even earlier. I remember that Khalid's mother had morning sickness for the full nine months. He was so tiny when he was born, just a skinny little thing with light wisps of hair on his head. You wouldn't know it to look at him now, though. Luqman was the first to walk. His mother was chasing him when he was just ten months old. Now he runs into the classroom, dancing around between the desks and never just walking. Rana was a quiet baby. Her mother was the envy of us all. I see that Rana is still quiet, sitting shyly at her desk, not participating in the giggling that has seized some her friends. Noora's mother teaches Arabic classes at the university. She was determined to have the smartest baby in the neighborhood, so she played tapes, in English and Arabic, to her child in utero. Now, while most of the boys bounce around the room and most of the girls talk and giggle, Noora sits at her desk, reading. Yes, I know them.

But I've never to tried to teach them or talk to all of them at once. Well, I'd better get started. "Assalaamu alaikum, class." Most of the girls and a few of the boys stop talking. There are still three groups of friends, though, who haven't yet acknowledged my presence. "I said, Assalaam alaikum," I repeat, in a firmer voice.

"Hey," Khalid shouts, "Yusuf's mom said to be quiet."

74

Khalid's come a long way from that skinny little newborn. He has a good set of lungs. The class settles down. They sit in their desks, waiting. It's my move.

"Thank you. I'll be your teacher for the next few days, so I hope we can have a good time together."

Noora puts down her book and raises her hand.

"Yes, Noora?"

"What happened to Sr. Asma?"

Before I can answer, Hashim yells out, "She doesn't want to teach since her husband got busted."

Hashim's family moved here when he was in second grade. I've never really liked that kid. Yusuf wants to go to his house sometimes, but I always insist that Hashim comes to our house instead so that I can keep an eye on him. He's always loud, and he likes to tease Amin, who usually ends up crying when Hashim's around.

"Remember to raise your hand, Hashim. Sr. Asma and her family are having some troubles right now, so she needs to stay home to take care of things."

"Sr. Sadia," it's Hashim again, "do you think Br. Uthman's a terrorist? My dad says he probably is."

It's going to be a long day. "That's not my business, Hashim, and I don't think we need to discuss it right now. I've known Sr. Asma and Br. Uthman for a long time, and I think they're good people. Right now we need to get to our reading lesson."

He starts to say something else, but I give him "the look" — the same look I've used on my own children many times over the last eighteen years. It works.

I fumble my way through the morning, faking it half the time. Fortunately, Noora helps me out.

"Sr. Sadia," she reminds me gently when I tell the class to line up and bring the jump ropes, "we have lunch first, and then recess."

"Oh, thank you, Noora." I smile, but inside I feel like a fool. I'm a college graduate, being advised by a ten-year-old.

In the afternoon they have social studies class. Finally, a subject I can identify with. I'm not going to teach them psychology, of course, but I do have a minor in history. I can handle this.

I look at the materials the principal gave me. The lesson scheduled for today is about the Revolutionary War. Yes, I know I can handle this.

I begin talking about the Patriots and the Loyalists. I note that about one-third of the colonists didn't really care whether or not they had independence from Britain. Chalk in hand, I carefully list the names of the leaders of the Revolution, working my way towards the battles.

I'm excited. I love this subject. It is afternoon, though, and I'm losing my audience. Some are staring into space, and two even have their heads on their desks. Yusuf is trying to look interested, but I can tell he's not really listening. Noora is the only one who appears to be learning anything.

I've been lecturing for about ten minutes when Khalid raises his hand.

"Yes, Khalid?"

"Can I go get a drink of water?"

"Yes, go ahead."

In the next few minutes eight other students ask to get water or go to the bathroom. I know what that means. I did the same thing in school when I was bored. It's time to change my approach.

I try to look excited, and clap my hands. The students startle. One of my sleepers actually sits up. "Okay, who can tell me who some of the leaders of the Revolution were?"

Noora raises her hand.

"Yes, Noora."

"George Washington led the troops. Thomas Paine wrote an important pamphlet called 'Common Sense.' And then there was ..."

I hate to do it, but I have to interrupt her. She's starting to put the class to sleep again.

"Okay, Noora, that's good for now. Let's talk about George Washington. Can anyone tell me what he was doing before the Revolutionary War?"

Noora raises her hand, but I want to give someone else a chance.

"I'm sure you know, Noora, but let's see who else can answer."

Yusuf raises his hand. I hope he knows.

"George Washington had been a surveyor. During the French and Indian War he was an officer in the British army."

"Very good, Yusuf." Thank you, Yusuf. You may have saved your mom today. "Okay, so George Washington was an officer in the British army. Now, who did the colonists fight against in the Revolutionary War?"

Luqman speaks up. "I think they fought against the British."

"Yes, Luqman, that's right. So, Washington fought with the British in the French and Indian War, and against the British in the Revolutionary War. What do you think about that?"

Rana, who's been quiet most of the day, raises her hand. "He must have really believed in what the Revolutionary War was all about."

Khalid waves his hand frantically until I call on him. "He must have thought that what the British were doing was wrong, and he needed to change it."

"Good. Those are both good answers. Yes, George Washington had fought with the British army, but when the ideas about a revolution began to spread, Washington became convinced that the British government was mistreating the colonists. He believed that the revolution was the right way to change things." The students are paying attention now. "Do you know what the British would have called him?"

Yusuf speaks up again. "He was a traitor." That comment wakes up my last sleeping student.

"Yes, Yusuf, to the British government he certainly was. In fact, those who participated in the revolution were aware of this. Benjamin Franklin once said, 'We must all hang together, or surely we shall all hang separately.'"

They have to think about that for a minute. Then Hashim yells, "Oh, I get it!" He laughs, and the rest of the class joins him.

I continue. "We can see that this country was founded by people who stood up for what they believed in. This is still an important value for all Americans."

Rana, who has been listening quietly, has a question. "Sr. Sadia, my parents are from Egypt. They moved to the United States when I was a baby. Am I an American?"

That's a good question. I pause before answering. "I know what you mean, Rana. How many of you have at least one parent who was born in another country?" About two-thirds of the students raise their hands. "In order to answer Rana's question, I think you need to ask yourselves some questions. Where is your home? Where do your friends live? Where do you feel most comfortable?"

Noora speaks up. "I feel comfortable here and in Syria. When I'm here, I'm with my friends. When I go back to Syria, I see my grandparents and lots of other relatives. Can I be both Syrian and American?"

"Sure you can, Noora. I'm sure many of you have different places that are special to you."

"Like me," says Luqman. "Both of my parents are American, but my mom is from Detroit and my dad is from Memphis."

Noora adds, "Well, wherever we are, we know that we are Muslims."

"Yes, Noora, we certainly are. We are all Muslims in America."

The bell rings, signaling the end of the school day. The students are all awake, and I think they actually learned something. I still don't want to be a teacher, but I guess I can do this for at least one more day.

On my way out, I'll ask the principal how close they are to finding a replacement.

CHAPTER FOURTEEN

The War

TEACHING IS AN amazing job. It both exhilarates and exhausts. While I am in the classroom with the fresh young minds, I feel excited, just being in the same place with all that energy. When I come home, I can barely move. I ask Salahuddin to bring dinner home from the restaurant.

The principal asks me to stay on until a new teacher is in place. I end up teaching for the rest of the week. On Tuesday, the principal tells me that someone is scheduled for an interview that afternoon. On Thursday morning, he says that she has been hired. On Friday she comes into the classroom to get acquainted with the students and their routine.

By Friday, I'm beginning to feel that this is "my class." I feel comfortable with the students, I know how to handle them and I can get through an entire day without reminders from Noora (though she's more than happy to help).

When the new teacher, Sr. Zainab, comes in and gets ready to take over, I'm almost sorry to see my time in the classroom end. The kids are so enthusiastic, and so innocent. When I'm with them, I absorb some of their energy. When I go home, though, I need a nap.

I spend Saturday catching up with the housework. In some ways, all these years, I've regretted not being out in the workplace, making my own place in society. On the other hand, I'm not sure I could manage it. The bathrooms are dirty, clothes are piled up by the washer, the furniture is dusty, and for the last two days I was so tired I didn't even hang up my clothes in the closet. They're still draped over a chair in our room. My kitchen is probably the cleanest room in the house because I didn't cook all week. I hope the kids won't miss eating restaurant food every night.

On Saturday evening Salahuddin drives me over to Asma's house. I called on Wednesday after school, but Aliya said that her mother was resting. When I get there, I find Asma sitting on the couch, wearing an old, faded dress. I visit for about an hour before Salahuddin comes to pick me up. During that time Asma's daughters greet me, offering some tea and small talk.

Farhia tells about the hundreds of men who were picked up in the first two weeks after the attacks. "Most of the men were Pakistani, too. I've been trying to get in touch with some of the other families, to see if we can help each other."

Uthman is not just loud and opinionated. He's also a statistic.

Asma is silent during the visit. Her face is expression-less. She listens to us, but she seems to be too tired to talk. She does smile faintly when I kiss her cheek before I leave.

"I've enjoyed my visit, Asma. Your daughters are such nice young ladies, and excellent hosts. I'll be back soon, insha Allah."

She nods silently.

I wish I could give her words of encouragement, telling her that Uthman will be home soon and everything will be all right. But I don't think she needs empty promises.

I didn't see Fareed during my visit. He was probably in his room. I wonder how he's holding up.

Sunday starts slowly. I take my time getting out of bed, make a late breakfast and sit down to read the paper. The day is quiet, a welcome change from the last few weeks. I hope that, just maybe, life will start to get back to normal.

I'm cleaning up from a late lunch when Adam calls me, "Mom, come here." He's watching television.

His voice sounds urgent, so I turn off the water, leave the last dirty dishes in the sink and go to see why he called. A news anchor is reading a statement. "Beginning at 12:27 p.m. Eastern time, U.S. and British forces began their bombardment of al-Qaida and Taliban forces in Afghanistan. About fifty cruise missiles have been launched against strategic sites in northern Afghanistan." The war has begun.

Adam looks pale. "Mom, what does that mean?"

Here we go again. Two times, in less than a month, I've had to talk to my boys about some of life's harsher realities. I can't think of any way to sugar-coat it. "Well, Adam, that means that the United States has begun its attack against Afghanistan."

"Why Afghanistan? Why do they want to hurt people there?"

"They say that Osama Bin Laden is hiding out in Afghanistan. The U.S. has told the Taliban to give them Osama Bin Laden, and they haven't done it. So the president decided to attack."

Adam looks puzzled. He's silent a moment, then asks, "What about Umayyah and Ubaydah?"

"Who?"

"You remember, Umayyah and Ubaydah. When we went to Seattle for vacation last summer. We met their father at the masjid, and he invited us to their house. They had a really good collection of Legos."

Yes, now I remember. Their mother, Zulaikah, fed us a delicious dinner, followed by tea and a special Afghani dessert. She was kind and welcoming, even though we were strangers.

"I remember them, Adam. What about them?"

"Umayyah told me that his father was going to take them all back to Afghanistan as soon as the Taliban got things under control. I guess they can't go back now, can they?"

The world is getting far too tough for children. "No, Adam, I guess they can't go back for a while at least."

Adam and I watch the news for a little while longer. I'm not paying much attention because I start thinking about Zulaikah's husband, Fawad. He's a medical technician at a major hospital. He speaks fluent English and his manners are refined, but he has a full black beard, and when we saw him, he was wearing a tunic top with baggy pants, the traditional Afghani dress. I wonder how he and his family will be affected by this news. It certainly won't be easy.

During dinner we talk about the war. Muhammad knows better than to complain about his football game being interrupted by the announcement, though that's probably what he's thinking. Yusuf leads the conversation.

"Mom, why do they have to bomb a whole country just to get one man?"

I try to answer thoughtfully. "It's not that simple, Yusuf. The U.S. government believes that members of the Taliban, who rule Afghanistan, have been helping Osama Bin Laden. If Osama Bin Laden planned the attacks, then the Taliban are guilty, too, aren't they?"

"I guess something like that happened to me," replies Yusuf. "Last year, when I helped Khalid cheat on that math test, we both got in trouble."

"Yes you did," says Salahuddin. "I hope you won't do that again."

"No, Baba."

Sadeq speaks up. "I was talking to a brother at the masjid who said that Osama didn't do it. You remember that, Baba. This brother said that the Israelis did it."

"I remember when he said that, Sadeq, and I'd like to agree with the brother when he said that Muslims had nothing to do with the attacks. But it's not right for us to blame someone else, either. Also, we have to be careful about throwing around all these theories. People say this and people say that, but we shouldn't say anything unless we're certain."

Sadeq starts getting defensive. "But, Baba, you know

that brother. You heard him too."

"Yes, I know who you're talking about. But I also know that we have to be careful. We can't just jump to conclusions."

I spot another teachable moment. Maybe my week in the classroom has made me more in tune with this.

"You know, boys," I say, "there have been a lot of instances when people have been blamed unfairly, not as individuals but as a group. Can you think of any?"

"What about the Native Americans?" says Yusuf. "Sr. Asma used to tell us how some of the people thought all Native Americans were bad."

"That's right, Yusuf. That's why some settlers called them 'savages.' Some people thought that Native Americans were wild, like animals. We know now, of course, that they were wrong."

Adam speaks up. "Br. Imran was telling us about slavery in class one day last week. He said that some people thought black people were like apes or something. Suleiman even said that his grandfather told him stories about how bad people treated him when he was young, and slavery was over by then."

"That's right, too, Adam. It's always bad when people see someone who's not like them and think they're all ugly or dangerous or stupid."

Muhammad, who has been eating quietly, breaks into the conversation. "I know what they should do to Osama Bin Laden."

"What?" I ask.

He grins. "They should change his name to Yusuf, and then put everyone named Yusuf in jail."

"Mom!" Yusuf yells.

"Muhammad." Salahuddin speaks sharply. "Aren't you getting to be too old for this nonsense? You have to set a good example for your younger brothers."

Muhammad looks down at the table. Salahuddin doesn't correct the boys often, but when he does they feel it.

Oh, Muhammad, when will you start to grow up? You're a senior in high school and you're still acting like a little kid.

"Really, Muhammad, what do you think should be done? If Osama Bin Laden was behind the attacks — though he may not have been — and the Taliban are protecting him from justice, what should the United States do?"

He looks up. "You know I don't like to discuss politics," yes, we all know that, "but, if I were in charge, I wouldn't bomb a whole country just to get one person. A lot of innocent people are going to get killed."

I agree, Muhammad. Maybe my football-loving, wise-acre oldest son will start growing up, after all.

CHAPTER FIFTEEN

The Big Scare

ON SATURDAY, THE day before the war started, I read a small article in the newspaper. It was interesting, but didn't seem to be significant. The article told about a man in Florida who had just died of anthrax. Authorities said that he had probably contracted the disease naturally, I think he was a hunter or something, and there were no indications that this was related to terrorism. I read the article, along with the rest of the paper, over breakfast, and then went on cleaning the house. It didn't seem to be that important.

I am surprised, then, when I pick up the paper on Tuesday and read that anthrax has been found in the man's office. Not only that, but another man in the same office has the disease. Still, the article treats the story as something minor. That was in Florida, after all, many miles away from here. It is only the last section of the article that concerns me. It's titled "Terrorist Link?" No, that can't be right. Please, Allah, not again.

Anthrax is mentioned in the news again on Wednesday. This time, there are reports of "white powder sightings" throughout the country. There's a separate article about how to handle suspicious packages. This is to be getting serious.

My mother calls on Wednesday night. First she asks about Salahuddin and the boys. Then she wants to talk about the anthrax scare that seems to be taking over the country.

"You know I don't usually get scared that easily, but some of my neighbors are really worried. Amanda told me that her husband got scared this afternoon when he found some flour she had spilled because, you know, the mail was sitting right there on the kitchen table next to the flour. He was about to call the police, but she stopped him in time. She'd been making cookies in the morning and hadn't cleaned up all the flour. I don't know, Sally. It is scary. What do you think?"

"Well, I'm like you, mostly. I don't want to overreact, either. But I have been getting the mail myself rather than sending one of the boys to do it. Isn't that silly?"

"Maybe not. Maybe this really is a terrorist attack."

"I don't know, Mom. It just doesn't seem like that to me. I think people are getting all worked up over nothing, just like Amanda's husband."

"I hope you're right."

Unfortunately, I don't think I am. Things are calm for a day or two, and then anthrax is showing up all over the place. There's a letter in Nevada, and another one sent to a network office in New York. By Sunday, a week after the bombing started in Afghanistan, the anthrax scare is almost as big a news story as the war. I even learn that there are two different ways of contracting anthrax. In fact, I know more about anthrax than I had ever wanted to know.

On Sunday there's a major story in the paper about anthrax being part of a terrorist attack. Great, just what we need. I'm already a little concerned about opening the mail. If fear about a terrorist attacks starts again, I'll have to be even more afraid about going out to the mailbox in my scarf. I'll probably never be able to set foot in a post office again.

The inevitable happens on Monday, when anthrax is found in a letter addressed to a senator. Senate offices have to be shut down, and the ventilation system is sealed off to prevent the spread of anthrax throughout the Capital complex. Hundreds of people working at the Capital are tested for anthrax.

There is a note enclosed in the envelope with the anthrax. It reads, "You cannot stop us. We have this anthrax. You die now. Are you afraid? Death to America. Death to Israel. Allah is great." Here we go again.

Salahuddin and I have been reading the papers and watching the news, but we haven't talked about the anthrax threat with our boys. After everything that's happened, I don't want to give them something else to worry about. That night at dinner, though, Adam brings up the subject.

"Mom, some of the kids in my class said something about anthrax. They said it's a disease, and that someone's been trying to kill people with it. How could they do that?"

I don't really want to talk about it, but at least I have another teachable moment. I have actually learned a lot about anthrax in the last week or so. "Well, Adam, anthrax is a disease. Usually it's carried by animals, and people don't get it unless they've been in contact with livestock or other animals, like moose or deer. The problem is that some people have died of anthrax because it was sent to them in the mail, in powder form. It looks like someone is using anthrax as a way to kill people. It's being called a biological weapon."

"But how can a disease be a weapon?" asks Yusuf. "You can't shoot it, like a gun."

"Well, people have been using diseases to kill their enemies for a long time. In the old days, even before I was born, they would take a diseased animal and throw it into the enemy's fort. The enemy soldiers would die from the disease."

"So the disease would kill people a lot more easily than guns would," says Sadeq.

Adam is frowning. "Who's spreading the anthrax? A couple of the kids said that Muslims are doing it."

"Like I always say," Muhammad remarks, "Muslims get blamed for everything."

Yusuf protests. "Sr. Zainab says that Muslims can't even cut down a tree or burn down a building when we're fighting with someone. And Muslims aren't even fighting with the United States. So how could Muslims be doing it?"

"I don't know," says Salahuddin. "That kind of fighting is for cowards. This time, I really don't think that Muslims are involved."

"Mom, how can we let people know that Muslims are really nice?" asks Adam. "Some people just think that Muslims like to crash into buildings and make people sick. How can we let them know how Muslims really are?"

I have to think about that for a moment. "Well, I guess we already do some things. Last winter, when we had that big snowstorm, Muhammad and Sadeq volunteered to clear Mrs. Robinson's sidewalk. Actually, they'll need to take care of her leaves this weekend, too. I almost forgot."

"Thanks, Adam," says Muhammad.

Oh, Muhammad. "Anyway, we can't control what other Muslims might do, or what people might think about Muslims. All we can do is to be good neighbors and good citizens. I would like to see you boys dress in a way that shows you're Muslims. With me, it's obvious, but you boys can hide behind your jeans and t-shirts."

"I have an Islamic t-shirt I wear sometimes," Sadeq says.

"That's a good start. It would be better, though, if you didn't wear those baggy jeans with it." I get up to put my plate in the sink. From the corner of my eye, I think I see Sadeq rolling his eyes.

Amin swallows a mouthful of mashed potatoes and makes his contribution. "I'm going to treat everyone nice, and then they'll be happy that I'm a Muslim." He grins and goes back to eating.

Everyone finishes his dinner and heads in a different direction. Muhammad goes to work, the other boys do their homework, and Salahuddin goes back to the restaurant. I'm stuck with kitchen duty. While washing the dishes, I think about our conversation at dinner.

Salahuddin comes home late. I wait until he gets settled. "There must be something else we can do. I want to get out into the community and make a difference."

He strokes his short black beard. "Reverend Wilson says that some of the ladies from his church go to the homeless shelter every week."

"I know that a lot of church groups do that, but I still don't feel safe getting out there in a strange environment. I'd probably get a wacko who has a thing against scarves. Besides, you won't even let me go to the grocery store by myself yet."

"You're right. The problem is, you want to get out there and help people, but it has to be some place that will be safe, even in these times. What about a school?"

"These days, I'm not even sure how safe schools are. Anyway, that week of teaching wore me out. I'd really like to do something with adults."

"You don't want to work with children, but you're afraid of working with adults. What's left?"

We sit there, thinking silently for a moment. Ah, I've got it. "I know. What about the elderly?"

"That's an idea. I don't think there's much violence in nursing homes these days."

"I'm serious. Do you remember when my Aunt Vivian was so sick and they had to put her in a nursing home for a few months before she died? I went to visit her when I was in San Diego that time. It was so sad, just being in that place. Some of the people looked so lonely. After I visited with Aunt Vivian, I ended up talking with another lady, too. She said that she was the last person alive in her family. Can you imagine?"

"No, I can't. Where I come from, we don't put people into nursing homes. When Ma and Pa get too old, they'll stay with one of my sisters."

"Well, in this country there are a lot of people in nursing homes. So, what do you think?"

"Go ahead and try it. At least you won't have to go through any metal detectors."

I hit him with a small couch pillow.

"Ouch! American women are so aggressive!"

CHAPTER SIXTEEN

The Visit

I SLEEP WELL and wake up before sunrise. After praying and sending the boys off to school, I go out to the patio to drink my coffee. The air is getting cooler, but the sun is shining and birds are singing. It's a beautiful day.

I call a local nursing home soon after their office opens. A woman answers.

"This is Mrs. Foster. How can I help you?" Her voice is light and friendly.

I blurt out the speech I've already prepared in my head. "Well, I was just thinking that I'd like to come out and visit some people in your home. I have five sons, ages 7 to 18, and I'd like to bring them with me, too, if that's okay."

Mrs. Foster answers in her same, sweet-sounding voice. "Yes, that would be very nice. When would you like to come?"

"Would Saturday morning be okay?"

"That would be good, as long as you come before eleven, because our residents eat lunch at eleven."

"Yes, I can do that."

"And what is your name?"

Every time I talk with someone I don't know, I have to decide which name to use. Legally, I'm Sally Abdullah. Occasionally, though, I go by Sally Pappas, my maiden name, and sometimes I go by Sadia Abdullah. I decide that this time I'd better let Mrs. Foster know who I am, so at least she won't turn me away at the door when she realizes I'm a Muslim.

"My name is Sadia Abdullah." Will she hang up on me now?

"Oh, that's a pretty name. So, Mrs. Abdullah, we'll be expecting you and your sons on Saturday at around, oh, 9:30?"

"Yes, that would be fine. Thank you, Mrs. Foster." Thank you for your kindness.

"We'll look forward to seeing you. Bye."

On Saturday morning I make sure that the boys are clean and nicely dressed before we head out. Muhammad and Sadeq aren't happy about going anywhere on a Saturday morning. They'd rather be sleeping.

We are met at the office by Mrs. Foster, a plumpish woman who has gold-rimmed glasses hung on a chain around her neck. "You must be Mrs. Abdullah," she says, with a smile and a handshake. "I'm so glad you could come. And, oh, what handsome boys." Amin giggles, Adam blushes and Sadeq rolls his eyes.

She leads us to the sunroom, where the residents are enjoying a nice view of a sunny day. "Some of our residents don't get many visitors," she explains as we walk down a long, wide hallway. "Just introduce yourself, and let the conversation flow. You may need to speak a little louder for some of the residents, but not for all of them. I'm sure that they will be happy to see you, especially this little one," she says, pinching Amin's cheek. He wiggles away and runs to me, holding tightly to my skirt.

All the boys, even my older ones, stay close to me. They need to assess the situation. I take the lead, approaching a thin, white-haired woman in a wheelchair.

"Hello, how are you today?" I say in a cheery voice. Maybe too cheery.

She looks at me and my boys. "Hi there," she says. "You have a nice group of young men here. Are they all yours?"

"Yes. Thank you. My name is Sally." I decide that it will be easier for her if I use a familiar name. My grandmother never did learn how to say "Salahuddin."

"I'm Emma Campbell," she says. "Are you from around here?"

"We've lived here for almost twenty years. I'm originally from California."

That seems to satisfy her. Unlike my appearance, my English is unmistakably American.

"How about you? Are you originally from this area."

"Oh, no. I grew up in South Dakota. Pa was a farmer. We lived near a small town, where I went to school in a one-room schoolhouse. When I turned sixteen, I became the teacher in that same school. It's torn down now, though, don't you know? I went back a few years ago. There are new houses where our farm used to be."

Miss Campbell continues with the story of her life. She was the second oldest girl in a family of six girls and seven boys. "Thirteen sure wasn't unlucky for my Ma and Pa," she says. "With the blessings of the Lord and a lot of hard work, nine of us were able to go to college."

After teaching in South Dakota for a few years, Miss Campbell says she convinced her parents to let her study at the state teacher's college. "It was called normal school in those days. At first they didn't want to let me go. They thought I might get swept off my feet by some dandy and forget all about my education. But I never did find a man who suited me."

I become so involved in the story of Miss Campbell's life that I completely forget about the time. Mrs. Foster startles me when she says, "I hate to interrupt, but it's time for us to get ready for lunch now." She raises her voice slightly (as I have for the last hour or so) and addresses Miss Campbell, "It's time for lunch now, Emma. This young lady and her boys will have to go for now."

Miss Campbell reaches for my hand and pulls me close. "You come again now, Sally. I had a really nice time talking with you today."

"Yes, Miss Campbell, I will."

"And bring those boys of yours. Especially the littlest one. He's just as cute as a bug. Aren't you?" She reaches over to Amin and pinches his cheek. He frowns, but doesn't pull away.

As Mrs. Foster wheels Miss Campbell off to lunch, I remember that I used to have five boys with me, not just one. I find the other four sitting at a table, talking excitedly with an old man in a thin grey sweater. Sadeq introduces me. "Mom, this is Mr. Phillips. He used to fight in World War II. He was just telling us about how he was taken prisoner in Singapore, where Baba's from."

"Nice to meet you," says Mr. Phillips. "I was telling these boys of yours how life was back in those days. Not many of us made it who were captured in Singapore. I went back there a few years ago with my wife, before she passed. It's a beautiful city now but, pardon my language, in those days it was more of a hell hole for me and my friends. No, not many of us made it."

I want to ask him more about his experience, but I'm interrupted by a nurse's aide. "Let's go, Ed. It's time for your lunch now. These handsome young men are just going to have to come back to visit another time."

Yusuf looks up at me, "Can we, Mom?"

"Yes, I think we can."

"Well, then, boys, I'll be talking to you later. Be good to your mother now, you hear."

"Yes sir," they mumble, suddenly shy again.

We watch Mr. Phillips walk slowly down the hall to the cafeteria, sometimes using the handrail.

"Well, boys, I guess it's time to go. We've got to get home so Muhammad and Sadeq can get ready for work, and it's almost our lunch time, too."

We walk quietly to the car, not wanting to disturb the silence of the halls. Before we reach the front door, Amin starts to skip and hum.

"Shh," whispers Muhammad.

When we reach the van, the boys start talking all at once. They want to tell me about Mr. Phillips and his adventures during the war.

"He said they had to go on long marches. Sometimes one of his friends would just fall down dead during the march, but the soldiers made him keep on marching," says Adam.

"He said that they almost starved. Sometimes all he had to eat was one bowl of rice a day, with no meat or anything," adds Sadeq.

"He said that before he was captured he actually killed some of the enemy," comments Yusuf, with wonder in his voice.

Muhammad speaks last, after his brothers have calmed down and had their say. "The strangest thing about him, Mom, is that he said he'd do it all again, even knowing how hard it would be. Can you imagine that?"

"Did he say why?"

"He said that war is a terrible thing, but it's important to fight for our freedoms. What do you think about that, Mom?"

"I don't know what to say." I truly don't. Some wars have been fought over petty differences or in the name of greedy leaders. For the "greatest generation," though, I guess World War II really was fought for our freedoms.

CHAPTER SEVENTEEN

Being a Woman

WHEN SALAHUDDIN COMES home, he's swamped with stories about our visit to the nursing home. Adam and Yusuf tell him all about Mr. Phillips and his experience in Singapore.

"Yes," says Salahuddin, "I remember learning about the fighting in Singapore. My mother was very young during the war, but she told me about the loud explosions. That's what she remembers the most. Also, she was afraid of the Japanese soldiers. My grandparents never wanted to talk about it. We learned about it in school, of course."

"Why didn't I ever learn about it?" asks Yusuf.

"The Japanese occupation of Singapore was part of my country's history. You learn about other events, such as the explorations of Lewis and Clark, because that's part of your country's history."

"Oh," says Yusuf. He seems satisfied, for now.

"Baba, can you teach us more about Singapore?" asks Adam. "Singapore is our country, too."

"Yes, I guess it is," says Salahuddin. "You're right. I'll try to remember to tell you more about Singapore. The last time we went to visit, Yusuf and you were very small. Amin hadn't even been born yet."

"That's no fair," says Amin. "I want to go to Singapore, too."

"We will again, some day. When they see you, your aunts are going to spoil you rotten."

I tell him about Miss Campbell, whom I consider to be

a true pioneer in the women's movement. "She refused to just accept what life had to give her," I state with admiration. "She went out to earn her own way."

"You sound almost jealous of her," Salahuddin notes. He knows me too well.

"Well, I guess, in a way. She was only eighteen when she went far away from her family to further her education —."

"Like you," he interrupts.

I continue. "Then she moved all the way to Chicago to take her first major teaching job. She took more classes at the University of Chicago, where she met many famous people. She's even traveled through Europe."

"Sadia, you're an educated woman. You don't spend time with famous people, but you have traveled to Singapore. Did you ask Miss Campbell about her family?"

"Yes. She never married, of course, but she has a special niece who takes care of her and comes to visit once a week."

"So, Sadia, would you rather spend your last years with a special niece or your five sons? Would you rather spend time with many famous people or one handsome husband?"

I don't respond. He waits patiently for a moment, then raises his eyebrows. "Well?"

"Don't rush me. I'm thinking." I pause. "By the way, when do I get the handsome husband?"

His beard tickles.

* * * * *

Khadijah and I have decided to go see Asma on Sunday afternoon. Because he's young and more trusting of the world, Imran is letting Khadijah drive by herself again. She's been going out by herself for the last two weeks or so. Because he hasn't seen any sign recently that he has to worry, my husband has agreed to let me go with Khadijah, without my usual male bodyguard.

Things have been quiet around town for the last month or so. In fact, we've seen even more kindnesses in recent weeks. I've heard that Muslims in some other cities are still having trouble, especially since the war began. I don't understand. The U.S. is attacking Afghanistan, but Muslims in the U.S. have to fear backlash from our fellow Americans because of the war. I once took a class in logic, but this one completely escapes me.

Khadijah comes by after lunch. As soon as she pulls her car into the driveway, I'm out the door, ready for freedom and companionship. Maryam, my best friend, is still in Texas. I like being with Khadijah, too. She's warm and open and, oh, so young.

"Assalaamu alaikum." I climb into her red compact. "How've you been?"

"Pretty good. Things at school are getting back to normal, at least. We had a police car in the parking lot when the war first started, but since nothing happened they've gone now."

"Yes, Adam mentioned that. It sure is weird, isn't it, how some people feel like blaming Muslims for the war in Afghanistan. At least nothing's happened around here."

"Actually, something did happen, yesterday at the mall." She must be surprised by the look on my face, because she quickly adds, "But nobody got hurt."

"That's good. What happened?"

"Sara called me last night and told me about it. She's one of our seniors, a very bright girl, and we've gotten pretty close because I've been helping her with college applications and finding scholarships."

I know Sara. She is a very nice girl, and she's also one of those students who's probably never had a B in her life. She and Muhammad have been in class together since first grade. Unfortunately, Muhammad has never come close to matching her. I keep telling myself that girls mature earlier than boys.

"So, Sara told me that she went with Zakia to the mall on Saturday. They had a nice morning, and bought some things. They were sitting in the Food Court eating lunch when some guys came up to them. Sara said they were probably in their early twenties. They started calling them all kinds of names."

"Let me guess," I interrupt. "Raghead?"

"That's one of them."

"Sand nigger, camel jockey. We all know the routine."

"Yes, we adults do. Remember, though, these are two teenage girls. Apparently, from what Sara said, the boys started getting vulgar, too."

"So what did Sara do?"

"She didn't have time to do anything. Before she could call for security, two of the boys attacked them."

I gasp.

"No, thank God, they weren't hurt. But the boys did grab the girls' scarves. Sara fought back and held on to her scarf. Zakia was so stunned, Sara said, that the boys were off running down the mall, waving her scarf, before she knew what had happened."

"That's terrible." I know Zakia, too. She's also been in class with Muhammad since first grade. Like Sara, Zakia is very smart. But Zakia lacks Sara's confidence. Even when she was a little girl, she was very shy. Her mother, who had her only child late in life, has always been very protective.

"As you can imagine, Zakia was extremely upset. Sara put her jacket over Zakia's head, and they went to the mall office to make a complaint. They'll probably never catch those boys, though, and if they do nothing will happen to them, anyway."

"I guess they would have had to actually hurt one of the girls before people would take notice."

"Yes, Sara was saying that the secretary in the mall office couldn't understand why Zakia was so upset. You know how sensitive Zakia is anyway, and apparently she was really sobbing. Sara tried to explain to this lady that a Muslim woman's scarf is part of her dignity. The lady still probably didn't understand."

"Probably not, since girls are usually trying to show more of their bodies, not less. My own mother still doesn't understand, and I've been a Muslim for over twenty years. 'You've got such pretty hair, Sally,' she says, 'why don't you show it off.' I tell her I do show it off — to Salahuddin. She'll say, 'But don't you want the rest of the world to know how pretty you are?' No, Mom, I want to say, not really. I don't even try, though, because I know she won't understand. It's just the culture."

"My own situation is a little different. When my mom became a Muslim, she decided not to cover, and she always told me that I didn't have to cover if I didn't want to. When I started college, though, I realized that I wanted people to know that I'm a Muslim, and that covering is part of my Islamic identity. At first she really didn't like it, because even all those years after her conversion she felt that covering was too submissive. I kept talking to her about it, though, and last year she decided to start covering, too. The next time she comes into town you've got to meet her. She's one of those women who covers with style."

"Like Asma."

"Yes. I hope Asma is starting to get her sense of style back."

As Khadijah says that, we pull up to Asma's house. Uthman was arrested in mid-September, and no one has thought to rake the leaves fallen from the large oak tree in the front yard. The girls are too busy, I'm sure, and Fareed has no one to direct him. I'll talk to Salahuddin about getting the boys over here to do it.

Aliya lets us in. The house is clean and well-organized, as usual. Asma is sitting on the couch — not stylish, but looking better than she has been. She doesn't seem to be crying much any more, but she still has dark circles under her eyes. I wonder if she's been able to sleep.

"Assalaamu alaikum," Asma says, as she rises to greet us.

"Walaikum assalaam," we reply, almost in unison.

"There's still no word." Asma says this in answer to our unspoken questions. "I know he's being held, but I don't know where. No charges have been brought against him. They won't let the lawyer see him. They're just keeping him somewhere, for whatever reason. Probably for having a big mouth." She tries to laugh, but her voice sounds scornful.

"Have you heard about the others?" Khadijah asks.

"Yes, I know about 800 Pakistani men who were arrested." She attempts another laugh. "Uthman brought me to this country to start our family. He said it would be an excellent place to raise our children. Now, where is the father?"

I want to ease the tension. "I remember when I first met you. Farhia and Aliya were tiny girls with their hair in braids. You always put the prettiest dresses on them every time you brought them to the masjid." Farhia and Aliya are sitting across from me now, young women who have returned to be daughters to their mother.

Asma smiles at her oldest daughters. "They were so pretty then, and they still are." She continues, "Uthman had a good job at the university. We thought we had a nice home and a safe place to raise our children. Our children were born here. They're Americans. But," she says bitterly, "their father is being called a terrorist."

Khadijah tries to be encouraging. "I'm sure that everything will turn out okay. The United States still has a system of justice that must be followed. It's wrong to hold someone without formal charges."

I wish I could share Khadijah's optimism, but I'm beginning to wonder if the system works as well as it used to. While I'm trying to decide if I should say this, Aliya speaks up.

"Three days before they came for Baba, one of my professors was also taken. He's also Pakistani. He was taken in almost the same way, in the middle of the night. Another professor told me that these things will become more common now. I think the system in broken."

It's sad to hear such cynicism from someone so young. She sounds just like Muhammad, though. When I was their age, I had thoughts of peace and love. Times do change.

Now I'd really like to change the subject. The atmosphere in the room is far too gloomy, even though the autumn sun is shining through the large picture window. "So, how are you holding up, Asma?"

She sighs and sits silently, not answering for a moment. The house is quiet, except for the sounds of the dishwasher running in the kitchen and the clock ticking on the living room wall. She stares into space. Maybe she's imagining happier days. Finally, she answers.

"I'm better. There are bad days when I can hardly get out of bed, and good days when I try to forget that anything is wrong. I felt so bad leaving those children. I loved being their teacher. But I couldn't do it anymore. It wasn't fair to them. I wish that I knew what to do. He's the one who brought me to this country, and now he's gone. I can't go back to my family, either, and leave Uthman here. It's so hard." She smiles. "I used to get so aggravated when he went into one of his rages. He was never violent, it was all talk. Now, I just wish he would walk through that door and go into one of his rages again. I want to hear him complaining about the traffic, the drivers, his students, his coworkers, the school, the house, anything. I just want to hear his voice." Tears roll down her face, but she remains quiet, composed. Aliya brings her some tissue.

I don't know what to say to Asma. I don't think there is anything to say. I turn my attention to the girls. "Aliya, how have you and your sister managed since coming home from college? Will you be able to transfer your credits?"

"I have a job. I'm working at the same store as Sadeq. Did he tell you? Farhia's still looking for a job. We've had our transcripts sent to the registrar here, and we're waiting to find out about our credits. But when I went to my dad's university last week, people treated me strangely. They know what happened, and I'm sure some of them think he's guilty. We may not be able to go there, either."

"What about Fareed? I never see him when I come."

Farhia shakes her head. "We're all worried about him. My mom and dad had an arrangement. She took care of us girls, and my dad took care of Fareed. Now that my dad's gone, Fareed is lost. He just spends all his time playing video games. We can't get him to help around the house, and he hardly comes out of his room. We're not sure how to handle him. I know yelling doesn't work, because I've tried that plenty. Like I said, he's lost."

"Why don't you let him spend some time at our house? He's in Adam's class, and he'd probably like hanging around with the older boys."

"That sounds like a good idea," says Farhia

"Next weekend then, okay? He can come home with my boys on Friday and we'll bring him back on Sunday."

"Thank you, Sadia," says Asma.

"It's the least I can do." It really is. I wish I could do more, like bring Uthman back to his family.

* * * * *

When I return home, Salahuddin is happy to see me, but not in the protective way he was before. I'm glad to see another sign that things might get back to normal, at least for our family.

"How was your visit?"

"Asma's still having a rough time." I tell him about the unraked leaves and the fatherless boy. He's happy to help in both causes. I don't tell him about the heartbroken wife. He probably wouldn't understand.

"Did you two have a nice ride together? Were there any more honking horns and name calling?"

I hesitate. Should I tell him about what happened to Sara and Zakia? If I tell him, it might make him more protective of me. If I don't tell him, he'll probably hear about it anyway. It is a small community. While I'm weighing the issue, he interrupts my thoughts.

"What's wrong, Sadia? Did something happen?"

Darn it! I forgot that he can read my face. I guess I'll have to tell him.

"The drive over was okay, but on the way there Khadijah was telling me about something that happened to two girls in Muhammad's class." I narrate the incident, pointing out that the girls weren't physically hurt, but that their dignity was tarnished.

He's silent for a moment. Finally, he says, "Being a woman must be really tough sometimes."

"Yes, it is. It's easier, though, for a woman who has an understanding husband."

His beard tickles.

CHAPTER EIGHTEEN

Maryam

I'VE MISSED MY best friend.

Maryam has been gone a little over a month. During that time the war against Afghanistan began and there was a panic over anthrax. It seems like she's been gone for a long, long time.

They come back into town on Sunday, while Khadijah and I are at Asma's house. She calls and leaves a message with one of the boys, but I know they've had a long drive so I wait until Monday morning to call back.

She answers the phone. "Assalaamu alaikum, Sadia."

They don't have caller ID. "How'd you know it was me?"

"Because I know the boys have left for school and you're ready to talk."

"You know me. I've sure missed you. So, how's Laila?"

"She'll be okay, but it's a good thing we went there. She was just starting to relax when anthrax came along. For a day or two she wouldn't let anyone get the mail. It just piled up in the box. She wouldn't let Yahya out of her sight."

"I can imagine. You remember how it is to be a young mother."

"Oh, I remember. Listen, Musa's calling me. I'll come over this afternoon and we can catch up."

"Musa's letting you drive by yourself?"

"You know Musa doesn't tolerate much foolishness. We drove all the way to Texas without any problem, and he figures that if something's going to happen, it will happen anyway. I'll see you in a few hours."

Now both Maryam and Khadijah are out on their own, leaving the house and driving themselves around without their bodyguards. I need to have a talk with Salahuddin.

Having Maryam back energizes me. I bake some cookies and marinate the chicken for dinner. While I work I day-dream about driving around town, without my bodyguards.

It's a little after 1:00 when Maryam comes. She looks good. "Oh, Maryam, I'm so happy to see you."

"You, too, girl!" I've missed her good, strong hugs, too.

She pulls back and looks me over. "Look at you. You lost some weight?"

"It's probably that week I spent teaching. Those kids really wore me out."

"You, a teacher? This I've got to hear."

We catch up over our tea and cookies. I tell her about my life in the last month, including Asma, Sara and Zakia, and my week of substitute teaching.

"Yes, I ran by to visit Asma on the way over here." I knew she would. "She looks pretty good today. She was wearing a nice dress and working around the house. She said, though, that she's got good days and bad days. It's a good thing she's got those girls to help her out. Tell me more about that teaching. You, a teacher? With a roomful of Yusufs? No wonder you lost weight."

"Well, they're really not bad kids. It's just that there's so many of them. One week was enough. So, tell me about your visit."

"That girl really needed some mothering. You know how it is when you're pregnant, and those hormones are racing at full speed." I nod. It's been seven years, but I remember. "Laila's got it bad. Between the new baby and this war on terror, she's going to drive herself crazy. While I was there, I had to be her mama all over again."

I guess we never outgrow needing our mothers. "So you had your work cut off for you, huh?"

"You're not fooling. At first we just had a nice time together. We went shopping for maternity clothes and new baby things. They want a girl this time, but she didn't buy anything pink just yet. I made her some of my special recipes, the ones she loved as a little girl. We talked, and talked, and talked. She took off a few days from work and showed me around the city. It was nice."

Maryam's been smiling, but her expression changes suddenly. "But then, do you know what that girl of mine wanted to do? She waited until after dinner one night, and brought us dessert, acting all nice and sweet. Then, she told us she wanted to stop wearing her scarf. 'It's so hard at work,' she said. 'People keep asking me questions. I'm afraid of what people will say about me.' She's been wearing the scarf since she was twelve, so you'd think it wouldn't even be a question for her. Apparently a couple of coworkers have been giving her a little trouble, over at the office where she works. Nothing serious, just enough to make her feel uncomfortable. And earlier that day someone had called her a 'raghead' for about the twentieth time since the attacks. She was ready to give up."

"What did you do?"

"At first I didn't have to do anything. Musa told her, gently but firmly, that she has to be able to stand up for her faith, pregnant or not. Her husband wasn't going to stop her. 'Oh, Baby, whatever makes you feel comfortable,' he said. Musa had a firmer talk later with him, in private."

"Did Musa's talk help her?"

"Of course, it did. She's his only little girl, and you know how daddies and daughters are. But I also had a quiet talk with her later, and I think that's what really made the difference."

Laila is a sweet girl, and I'm beginning to feel sorry for her. "Like you said, Maryam, it is hard being pregnant. With this war on terror and all, I guess you could understand how she feels."

"That's just the point. I do understand how she feels."

She pauses a moment, and sighs. "Ibrahim was born in 1968, just two months after the assassination of Dr. King. We were living in Detroit at the time, and Musa was on the police force there. Do you remember the riots that broke out after Dr. King's assassination?"

"Yes, I vaguely remember. I was only ten years old."

"It was bad. There were lootings, cars being burned, rocks being thrown and fires being set all over the city. Musa had to be out there, night after night, trying to keep the peace. There I was, waiting at home alone with a little boy in diapers and another one on the way, and never knowing if Musa would make it home each night." She's always so stoic, but her voice starts to quiver with the memory.

"So that's what you told Laila."

"Yes, that's what I told Laila. Sure, she's got a hard time right now with the war and the anthrax and all. But back in '68 Musa and I had to struggle every day to stay alive and keep our family safe. He was out there on the streets every night. What Laila fears isn't the reality of danger, like what her father and I faced, but the possibility of danger."

We're silent for a moment. I've known Maryam for almost twenty years, but she's never told me about this part of her life.

She continues. "When Ibrahim was a few months old, we had a chance to move here. Musa wanted to get us out of the city. Even when we came here, though, we had problems. This town wasn't very open to black people in 1968. Musa was the first black man on the police force, and we were the first black family on the street. Right after we moved in, about five houses on the block went up for sale. When Ahmad started school, he had to put up with a lot — there were only two other black kids in the entire school. By the time Laila came along, though, things were starting to get easier. By the time she started school, it wasn't so strange to see a black face among the white. She just hasn't had to deal with too many difficulties before. Now, when problems do come along, Laila and her husband both are ready to do whatever it takes to get by.."

"So you and Musa set them straight."

"We sure did. We should have told her these things long ago. I didn't realize, until we started talking, how much she didn't know about those days when her brothers were little. By the time she started school, Dr. King had already been dead ten years. There were black faces on TV and in the government. I hadn't realized how different things were for her generation."

"You know, I can kind of identify with Laila, even though I'm older than her. It's hard when you grow up in a country and then, one day, you're looked at as a potential terrorist."

"Then I need to tell you what I told Laila. I said, 'Girl, you're worrying about the wrong things.'"

"How is that?"

"You know that I was in the Nation of Islam back in the early '60s. We followed the teachings of Elijah Muhammad and listened to the speeches of Malcolm X. When he came back from hajj as Malik El-Shabbaz, we followed him in that path, too. The thing is, back in those days anyone associated with the movement was pretty much considered to be a terrorist."

"Yes, I remember that. Lots of white people thought that black people would try to rise up and overthrow the whole white society. My own parents were worried. They weren't bigoted, but all that talk about Black Power made them nervous. They saw the rioting and looting on TV and, yes, they did think that most black people those days were terrorists."

"And yet I just got through telling you about how Musa and I were not terrorists, but terrorized by the things that were going on in those days. Sound familiar?"

"The more things change, the more they stay the same, I guess."

"I guess."

We talk and talk, catching up for lost time. Soon it's

time for the boys to come home. We hear their noises first — car doors slamming, voices raised, athletic shoes slapping against the pavement. They bounce in through the back door. Amin runs to Maryam. "Sr. Maryam, you're back. Did you bring me something?"

"I sure did." She pulls a piece of candy from her purse. "There you go, just for you."

The others straggle on through. Yusuf gets a piece of candy. The older boys just smile and greet her softly before heading up to their room. As usual, Adam lingers in the kitchen.

"You're getting big, Adam," Maryam says. "I guess you're just about too old for me to hug you. How've you been? How's school? What are they teaching you these days?"

I usually get short, noncommittal answers to such direct questions. Maryam's special, though.

"Lots of things. In science we'll get to dissect a frog next week. In English we're learning how to write short stories. We've been playing basketball in P.E. And, oh, in social studies today Br. Imran wanted to talk to us about the war and stuff. He said these are interesting times. Did anything interesting happen when you were young, Mom?"

Maryam and I both laugh. "I grew up in very interesting times," I say.

"What happened?"

"Well, there was the Vietnam War, some assassinations, race riots, peace protests. Something was happening all the time."

"I was talking with your mom about what I was doing in the '60s, while she was growing up. Do you know about the civil rights movement?"

"Yeah, we learned something about that last year."

"Br. Musa and I were in the middle of it, for a while at least. Back before Ahmad was born, we were down in Alabama marching for voting rights. Did you know that in some places it was almost impossible for black people to vote back then?"

"That wasn't right," says Adam.

"No, it sure wasn't. Then, in '63, Musa and I rode the bus to Washington, D.C. to hear Dr. King speak."

"You heard Martin Luther King?" Adam is clearly impressed. So am I.

"I sure did. I knew that very day that things were going to turn around. All that energy in one place. Dr. King was a very important part of that, but there were many others who aren't well known. Some of them died before the fight was finished. We all owe them our gratitude."

"But wasn't the civil rights movement just for black people?"

"At the time it was mostly for black people, Adam, because we needed it the most. But it was really for everyone. If one group of people in the society is oppressed, then the whole society will be weaker for it."

"I never thought of it that way," says Adam.

Neither have I.

CHAPTER NINETEEN

War and Peace on the Homefront

I SHOULD BE happy. My best friend is back, and we just spent a really nice afternoon together. But I'm not happy. My mood is gray, and it darkens as afternoon darkens into evening.

We eat dinner without Salahuddin. He said that he'd have to work late today. The boys carry on a conversation about something. I'm not paying attention. I'm brooding over the something that's bothering me.

After dinner I send the boys upstairs to do their homework, and I stay to do the dishes. I rub each dish a little harder than necessary. Yes, I'm angry. Why am I angry? Because Salahuddin is still trying to protect me. His form of protection feels like bondage. I'm shut up in the house, never allowed to run simple errands by myself, never allowed even to drive down the street for a gallon of milk by myself.

He's later than usual. This gives me more time to think. Even before the attacks he was becoming more protective, more controlling of my time and movements. He wasn't like that when we were first married. When the kids came along, I accepted a certain loss of freedom as part of the job description. But the kids are all in school now, and I'm locked up like a princess in a tower.

By the time Salahuddin comes home, the younger boys are in bed, and the older ones are winding down. When he walks in, I'm sitting on the couch, fuming.

"Assalaamu alaikum, Sadia. You're usually in bed by now."

"Are you trying to tell me what time I should go to bed now? Is that something else you want to control?"

He looks stunned. What a faker.

"No, I'm not trying to control anything. I was just saying ..."

"It's always about you, isn't it? What you want, what you think, what you say." I'm starting to shout.

"Sadia, settle down. You're going to wake up the boys." His voice is still annoyingly calm.

"Stop telling me what to do. Why are you always so damned calm all the time? You're always in control. You always want to control everything. I'm tired of living under your control."

He's biting his lower lip. He always does that when he's upset. It's always the lip first, and then the voice. Not yelling, but tense. "Sadia, I want you to stop this. I come home from a long day at the restaurant, and I expect to come home to a peaceful household. Your behavior is out of line."

"It's always my fault, isn't it? You never take any responsibility."

"Responsibility for what?"

"You should know. You don't pay any attention to me at all. You don't even know what I need." I start crying. The tears are real, representing all these months of frustration.

"What the hell am I supposed to know?" Now he's shouting.

I stop. Salahuddin never curses. Never. But I can't stop. I try to talk, between my sobs.

"You're supposed to know that I have to get out of the house."

Now he stops. He stops biting his lower lip, and starts to laugh. "Is that all? Is that what this is about?"

I hate it when he laughs like that. "What do you mean, is that all?" I yell. "How would you like being locked up in the house all day? I can't go anywhere. I just cook and clean, clean and cook, day after day. Do you want me to be your little Barbie doll in your little dollhouse? Because that's how I feel."

Before he can answer, we hear a small voice in the doorway. "Mom, is something wrong?" It's Amin.

"Oh, no, sweetie. Everything's okay. Come on, Mama will take you back up to your bed." As I walk toward the stairs, holding Amin's hand, I glare back at Salahuddin. "I think Baba wants to sleep down here tonight."

I sleep well. I finally let out my frustrations.

When I go down to get some breakfast for the boys, Salahuddin is still asleep on the couch. "Why is Baba sleeping down here?" Yusuf asks.

"Oh, I guess he was watching TV and he just fell asleep."

Muhammad and Sadeq exchange knowing glances. They know too much.

"Wake up, Baba," says Amin. As Salahuddin slowly become conscious, I duck into the kitchen. Let him come to me this time.

The other boys are almost finished eating breakfast when Adam walks in. "Hey, I'm not late today!"

I glance at the kitchen clock. "Actually, you are late. It's just that your father's late, too."

"Really? Baba's never late." Adam grabs a bowl from the cupboard. "I finally get to eat breakfast."

Adam is almost finished with his cereal when Salahuddin walk in. He looks at me, but I pretend to be interested in the writing on the back of the cereal box. From the corner of my eye, I see him frown.

"Go to the car now, boys. I need to talk to your mother for a minute."

Muhammad quickly herds his brothers out the back door.

"But I'm not finished," says Adam.

"Too bad. Now get going." Muhammad is the last to leave. He glances over his shoulder on the way out.

Salahuddin waits until Muhammad is out of sight before he speaks. His hair is slightly out of place, and he has circles under his eyes. He looks more handsome to me now, when he's not so perfect. I catch myself. Careful, Sadia. Hold your ground.

I'm still pretending to read the cereal box when he starts. He speaks softly. "I didn't sleep much last night, which is strange because I was very tired when I got home. I was trying to think what would make you act like that." I'm tempted to say something, but I don't want to start another fight. Maybe I should just listen. He continues. "I finally figured it out. You're right. You have been a prisoner since the attacks. It's not fair, and it's not my fault, either. It's the people. The ones who vandalized the restaurant, who shot that brother in Dallas, who harassed the girls in the mall. It's their fault, not mine. And not yours."

He does understand. I want to hug him, but I can't give in. Not yet. "You're right about the people," I say, "but it's not everyone. Just like it wasn't every Muslim who brought down the towers. There are many types of people out there. Some are very kind. We have to be able to trust someone, sometime. And I can't stay a prisoner."

"I know you can't. But I can't let anything happen to you." He pauses. "You mean so much to me."

Okay, he's got me now. I put down the cereal box and hug him. "Thank you." We hold each other for a moment. Then I pull back.

"Salahuddin, Maryam drove over here by herself yesterday. She's been going out by herself for weeks now. So has Khadijah. You have to trust me to handle things. You have to trust in Allah."

He winces. "You're right. Not today, though. What about this?" He pauses, putting his thoughts together. "Let's see how things are for the rest of the week. If nothing bad happens in this so-called war on terror, no attacks or threats against Muslims, you can go."

I guess that's the most I can ask for. "Okay. On Saturday?"

"Sure. Now, I'd better get those boys off to school."

His beard tickles.

* * * * *

When they come home in the afternoon, Salahuddin makes a show of kissing me in front of the boys. They say it's important to let the children know you've made up, and Salahuddin takes care of that.

He also makes sure he's home for dinner. He may be afraid to work late for a while.

"Mom, something happened at school today," Adam says, in between bites of meatloaf. "There was a fight."

"Yeah, you should have seen it," says Sadeq.

"What happened?"

"Fareed and I were walking to our Arabic class. We were almost there when a sixth grader came up to Fareed and called his dad a terrorist. He said, 'I hope your dad stays in jail.' Fareed just jumped on the kid." Adam narrates with embellishment.

"That kid deserved it," says Yusuf. "He's bad. He's always picking on the fifth graders, and then trying to get us in trouble."

"Man, I didn't know Fareed could fight like that," says Sadeq. "He had that kid on the floor. The kid only got in one good punch to the ribs. Fareed pounded him."

"Weren't there any teachers around?" Fighting in the hallways? This is why I send my kids to a religious school?

"Not at first," says Adam. "Then Br. Imran heard the noise and came out of his room. Br. Faruq came out of the Arabic classroom, too. Br. Imran took hold of Fareed and Br. Faruq took care of Bassam."

Oh, it was Bassam. That kid's been a handful since he was in preschool. I don't understand it. His parents are so nice.

"Anyway," Adam continues, "I went into Br. Imran's classroom for a minute, just to see how Fareed was doing. It took a long time for Fareed to get quiet. His face was all red. He was really mad. I thought he might even hit Br. Imran."

"Man, then he really would've been busted," says Sadeq.

"Then Br. Imran told me to go to class. By the time I got to Arabic class, Bassam was already in the principal's office. They had a meeting after school, with Fareed's mom and Bassam's parents. I think they got suspended."

"Was anybody hurt?"

"No, except I think Bassam might have a black eye."

Salahuddin has been listening quietly. "Boys, what do you think about what Fareed did? Was it right?"

"No, but I would have done it, too," says Muhammad. "That kid was dissing his dad."

"Thanks for the support, Muhammad, but I don't want you getting into any fights. Fighting isn't the right way to handle things."

"Then what were you and Mom doing last night?"

I am going to smack that boy. I don't hit my kids, but some day I'm going to smack that smirk right off his face. He looks at me, and senses the danger.

"Sorry, Mom. Sorry, Baba."

I don't know what to say. It's frightening when your children know you that well.

"I'll fight for you too, Baba."

"Thank you, Amin." Salahuddin chuckles and shakes his head. Sometimes you just can't win.

After the table is clear and all the food is put away, I call Asma.

"Assalaamu alaikum, Asma. How are you holding up?"

"You heard? About my son? His father would be so ashamed."

"Well, at least he was trying to defend his father." I don't say that Fareed must have inherited his father's temper, but Asma seems to hear my thoughts.

"Uthman was a lot of talk, but he never hit anybody. Never. I don't know what to do with Fareed. I want to scream at him, and then I feel sorry for him. Just like I feel sorry for myself." She pauses, then continues. "He's been suspended for a week. I don't know what to do with him. Of course, he can't come to your house next weekend."

"Actually, Asma, I think you should let him come. Salahuddin can keep him busy helping out around the house, or over at the restaurant. He needs someone."

"I know. So do I."

I feel guilty, and grateful, to have a husband I can fight with. Asma doesn't even have that.

* * * * *

Asma thinks about it for a couple of days, and finally agrees to let Fareed come to our house on Friday night, as we had planned before the fight.

Salahuddin makes plans to keep the boys occupied during the weekend.

The week has passed without any major incident. There are more anthrax incidents, and the war in Afghanistan continues, but these are becoming common occurrences. Tomorrow morning I'll be able to go out on my own.

When I go with Muhammad and Sadeq, they're completely unintrusive, because teenagers understand the need for privacy better than anyone. Still, I'm looking forward to being alone. I can browse through the bookstore without a couple of bored teenagers waiting for me to finish, or I can go window shopping in every store of the mall. Finally, I'll be free.

Asma brings Fareed over before dinner time.

"You behave yourself, Fareed. I don't want any more trouble. Let me know, Sadia, if he gives you any problems. I'll come get him right away."

"I'm sure he'll be fine, Asma. Don't worry."

"Just call me if you need me." She's looking good today, dressed as stylishly as she was before Uthman was taken away. "And tell Salahuddin 'thank you' for taking on another boy."

"It's no problem, really." I laugh. "With boys, you just

throw them all together and stand back to watch the fun."

"Okay, if you say so." Asma gives me a strange look, and shakes her head as she walks back to her car.

We have a quiet dinner. Fareed, normally a loud, outgoing boy even before his father went away, sits shyly. "May I have some more rice please, Sr. Sadia?"

"Yes, of course. Would you like some more chicken, too?"

"Yes, please." I pass him the chicken platter. He chooses a leg quarter. "Thank you very much."

My own boys looked surprised at this change in Fareed. Asma prepared him well.

"Fareed," says Salahuddin, "we're going to be splitting up chores tomorrow. What kind of work do you do around your house?"

Fareed lowers his eyes. "Um, I don't really do much of anything at home. My sisters do all the cooking and cleaning and stuff. But I used to help my dad fix things."

"That's good enough. We've got a lot of fixing to do, between here and the restaurant. After working, maybe we can go out for ice cream. Does that sound good?"

"Yes, Br. Salahuddin, I'd like that." He smiles.

On Saturday morning I'm smiling. I get up and dressed, ready for my day out.

"Be careful," Salahuddin says as I head out the door.

"I will. Have fun, you and your workers." I walk out, the storm door slamming behind me. I'm free.

I climb into my green compact. I haven't driven this car since before the attacks. Every time I've gone out, I've been stuck with the van. Muhammad has practically taken over my car. When I get back, I'll make him clean out the soda cans and fast food wrappers.

I pull out of the driveway and head down the street. My first stop will be the bookstore.

CHAPTER TWENTY

Ramadan in a Time of War

RAMADAN IS COMING, and things are looking up.

I come home safely from my trip, with no harrowing tales to tell, and Salahuddin appears to relax. Over the next week or so he becomes less cautious about letting me go out. After two weeks it feels normal, as it was before the attacks.

Fareed spends every weekend with us. A few times Adam and he started to fight, but it was over petty things, the kinds of things brothers fight over. Salahuddin's been spending a lot of time with him, and I can see the slouch disappear from his shoulders.

Asma is getting her self back. She's dressing nicely, and has started volunteering a couple of days a week at the school. She talks less about Uthman, too. All of us, my close friends and other mothers at the school, still wonder where Uthman is and what will happen to him. Some are starting to wonder if he really is a terrorist.

It's been almost three weeks since my liberation, and Ramadan begins. We start fasting on a Friday.

I've been getting ready for Ramadan for several days now, buying special food and keeping the house spotless. A local reporter interviewed some Muslims in the area, asking how Ramadan would be different this year. Most had the same message as our imam, who said, "Ramadan is always a special month. The terror and difficulties of the last two months will make it more special." I agree.

For many Muslims, Ramadan is a time to spend with

the community. They go to the mosque every night to break the fast, sharing the experience with many others. Sometimes, our family does this, too, but our emphasis is on family time.

On Thursday night Salahuddin takes Muhammad, Sadeq and Adam to the mosque for special prayers. I wake up early Friday morning, long before sunrise, to fix a special breakfast.

"Let's go, boys," I yell up the stairs, "come eat suhur. I've got cinnamon rolls, hash browns and eggs. Come on. You've got about thirty minutes before dawn."

The first morning is the easiest. They come eagerly down the stairs, ready to stock up before the day of fasting ahead. The next thirty minutes is a blur of food, boys and noise. Then, a recording of the adhan rings out from a special clock we have, and it's time to stop eating and drinking for the day.

Yusuf is ten, and this Ramadan he'll try to fast every day for the entire month. Last year he fasted about every other day, and he's been fasting for at least a few days each Ramadan since he was seven. Amin just turned seven , but I don't think he's ready to fast yet. I talked to him about it a few days ago.

"Amin, you're getting to be a big boy now. How many days will you fast this Ramadan?"

"I can fast every day if I get to eat lunch, too."

The first day passes quickly. The boys come home from school after the Friday prayer. My older boys rest, while Yusuf and Amin go watch TV. Actually, it's an Islamic cartoon video. During Ramadan I restrict TV to the news only. Some families don't allow any TV or videos during the month.

While the video plays, Amin comes to the kitchen for some crackers and cheese. He does this almost every afternoon, so I don't pay attention. Soon, though, I hear, "Mom!"

It sounds urgent. I run into the living room. Everything

looks okay. "What's wrong, Yusuf?"

"Mom, Amin's eating in front of me. He can't do that."

Amin puts on his cutest grin. "I'm sorry, Amin. Yusuf's right. Why don't you come eat in the kitchen?"

"But, Mom," says Amin, "I want to watch the video."

"In the kitchen, Amin. Now." He follows me, unhappily. Yusuf is grinning.

Salahuddin comes home an hour before sunset, when we'll break fast. During Ramadan he opens his restaurant only during the day, so both Yaqub and he can use the evening to be with family, read the Qur'an and say extra prayers.

I finish dinner preparations and sit down to read Qur'an with them. While we read, the clock ticks slowly. There are thirty minutes left, then twenty, then ten. In the last minutes Yusuf helps me set up the food. First, we bring out the water and dates. This is what Prophet Muhammad used to break his fast. I've also made a special dessert.

The times comes. Amin makes the adhan, while we say short prayers and take grateful sips of water. There's a moment of silence, and then noise as the boys begin eating dates and dessert.

"Do you think you'll be able to fast the whole month this year, Yusuf?" Salahuddin asks.

"I don't know. I got kind of hungry after school. And Amin ate in front of me. But I want to fast. I don't know yet."

"You're getting to be a big boy, but you're still young enough to break your fast if it gets too hard."

"Why does it have to be twelve whole hours?" Yusuf complains.

"You're lucky," I say. "When I became a Muslim, my first Ramadan was in July. We had to fast for about sixteen hours, and it was hot. Now the days are short and cool. But like your dad said, you don't have to fast if you don't feel well."

"Why do people want to fast?" Amin asks.

"Ramadan is a special month," I say. "The Qur'an was

revealed in Ramadan. We believe that there are special blessings during this time. Remember, too, that the prayers you say when breaking fast are very important. Allah loves the prayer of a fasting person."

"Yeah," says Adam. "Last year I prayed every day for a new bike, and on Eid I got one."

What will I pray for this year? Last year I said general prayers for my family and friends. This year is special, though. I need a special prayer.

The days pass quickly. Sometime during the first week I decide to pray simply for peace. It sounds so trite, but it's so badly needed. The peace I pray for isn't just the absence of war. It's a state of existence in which war is no longer necessary. It seems impossible, but Adam's new bike also seemed impossible to him. There are moments when I think I must be wasting my time, but I keep on praying anyway.

Thanksgiving Day comes during Ramadan this year. We usually fly out to California to celebrate Thanksgiving with my family, but I don't think we'll make it this year. I've been putting off telling my mother we wouldn't come, and I finally call her less than two weeks before Thanksgiving.

"I wish you could come, Sally. Your brother and sister will be here, with all their kids. Aunt Liz is coming, too, all the way from Santa Clara."

"I know, Mom. I'd like to be there. But it's Ramadan now, and it's hard to travel when we're fasting. Besides, I'm not sure I even want to get on a plane these days."

"What happened? You were always the risk taker of the family."

"I know, Mom, but things change. I don't think there will be another terrorist attack, but who knows?"

"You're a Muslim. You're supposed to know when the terrorist attacks are coming."

"Mom! You don't mean that, do you?"

She's laughing. "No, of course not. It was just a joke. You haven't lost your sense of humor, have you?"

Maybe I have. "No, I guess not. Just say hi to everybody for me, okay. I'll call on Thanksgiving Day and talk to everyone."

"Okay, then." She's using that tone of voice, the one she used when I told her I was going to major in psychology instead of business, but not quite the one she used when I told her I was going to become a Muslim and marry Salahuddin.

We don't do anything for Thanksgiving. The school is closed because most parents are off from work, and families want to be together. Salahuddin keeps his restaurant open for the few customers who want something other than turkey. The boys play and sleep most of the day. I spend an hour talking to my family in California, and make a simple dinner.

I would cook a turkey, but it's almost the middle of Ramadan and our appetites have decreased. That always happens when we fast. During the day, the food looks so good. When it's time to break fast, though, just a little is enough. Ali sells turkeys at this time of year, so I ask him to reserve one for me. I'll cook it on Eid day.

A few days after Thanksgiving, anthrax is found on a letter mailed to an elderly woman, who died a week or two ago. There's another suicide bombing in Israel. Sixteen people die and, of course, "Islamic militants" are to blame. The city of Kandahar falls to American forces in Afghanistan, but Osama Bin Laden escapes. An even larger battle takes place a little while later in Tora Bora, but Osama Bin Laden still can't be found. In my heart, and in my home, Ramadan has brought a feeling of peace. In the world, it's violence as usual.

Sometimes it's very hard to fast every day. Still, when the fast is over at the end of the day, I remember it as being easy. The hardest time of the day for me is the morning. I try to get up every morning to make an early breakfast for my family. There are some days, though, when we have to go back to cereal and the toaster.

Ramadan passes. Hour by hour, day by day, it slips away, and soon it's almost gone. After dinner one evening, near the end of Ramadan, Salahuddin and I talk about giving our money to charity. Every year, every Muslim is required to give some money to the needy. Salahuddin and I, like most other Muslims, prefer to do this during Ramadan. We've always sent the money overseas, to help Muslims in other countries.

"I want to send the money to Afghanistan this year," I say. "You've seen the pictures. People there were already suffering before the war, and now it's even worse. Many of them have lost their homes and members of their families. They deserve it more than anyone this year."

"You're right, Sadia, but we can't do it. It's just not safe."

"But we have to give the money to those who need it most. Who is needier than the Afghan people right now?"

"Do you know how many Islamic charities have had their accounts frozen in just the last two months? If we send money overseas through an Islamic charity, we may find our personal accounts frozen, too. If we give money to a charity that's suspected of terrorist ties, they could even shut down the restaurant. We don't know, either, which charity will come under suspicion next. They look good to us, but the next day they may be labelled as supporting terrorists."

"That's not right."

"No, but that's the way things are. I don't want to risk our assets. It's just too dangerous."

"I guess you're right. Nothing makes sense any more. This isn't the country I grew up in."

"No, but we can't spend our time looking back. We have to deal with the current situation. Let's just give our money locally this year. I'm sure we can find people who are in need right here in our town."

"That's safer, I guess, and we can still help someone. I

guess we don't have any other choice."

The next day Salahuddin contacts the imam, who helps us find families who are truly needy. In one of the families the parents are recent immigrants who have six children under the age of ten. Another family is in need because the father was just laid off from work. Salahuddin and I go together that evening to deliver the money and some food. I'm happy we could help. I keep praying, too, that someone will be able to help the people of Afghanistan.

Throughout the month I've been quietly buying Eid gifts for my boys and hiding them in my closet. On the last Wednesday of Ramadan I take the boys out after school to buy them new clothes for Eid. Yusuf and Amin are easy to buy for, but we have to go to four different stores before Sadeq finds something he likes.

Different families have different traditions for Eid. In our family we start with a big breakfast. There's no fasting on Eid, so we don't have to watch for the dawn today.

After breakfast we all get dressed up in our new clothes. The boys look so handsome. We take a few pictures, then get in the van to go to Eid prayer.

There are over a thousand people at the prayer, more Muslims than I ever see at any other time of the year. I'm still getting used to the sight and sound when Maryam emerges from the crowd.

"Assalaamu alaikum, girl. Eid Mubarak!" She hugs me tightly.

"Eid Mubarak to you, too." She's wearing a light blue tunic with pants. "You look good. Where'd you get that outfit?"

"I picked this up in Dallas. I also bought little Yahya a navy suit for Eid. Wish I could be there to see him in it. I like your dress, too. You look good in that shade of green."

We hold hands and make our way through the crowd, greeting other women and trying to get to the front. It's good to be sitting near the front during the sermon because there are always women talking in the back.

Khadijah's already sitting in the front row. "Hey, you two, over here."

"Assalaamu alaikum. Eid Mubarak," we call out.

"Eid Mubarak to you two, too." There's no more time to talk for now, because the imam is getting ready to lead the prayer.

After the prayer and the sermon it's always the same. Everyone is greeting and hugging. This is our happiest day of the year. The fast is over, and now it's time for the feast.

Khadijah and Imran invite us to come over for brunch. We plan to stop in for an hour or so before heading home.

Asma is there. "Assalaamu alaikum, Asma. I didn't see you at the prayer. You must have been lost in the crowd."

"No, I didn't go. Some people think he's guilty, you know. I didn't want to face them. Besides, Uthman always loved Eid. I keep wondering what he's doing today, and I don't think I can enjoy myself while he's locked up. I'd rather just stay in bed and forget about Eid, but I have to think of my children."

Her girls look lovely as they help Khadijah serve the brunch. Fareed looks good in his suit, but he's slouching again. I should invite them all over to our house, but I'm feeling selfish today. I want to have the day to myself and my family. I'm not very proud of myself right now.

Salahuddin comes over and whispers in my ear, "Let's invite Asma and her family over for dinner. There will be plenty of food."

"Okay," I say in a quiet voice. I have my own Jiminy Cricket, but mine is a little taller and has a beard.

We invite Asma to come at four. That gives me a few hours to give the boys their presents and get dinner ready. The turkey is still marinating in the refrigerator.

We stay for a while, then politely excuse ourselves. The boys are anxious to get their Eid presents, and I've got to get that turkey into the oven.

Once the presents and the turkey are taken care of, we

spend the rest of the afternoon playing and resting. Asma and her children come promptly at four.

"Thank you for inviting me, Sadia. It means a lot."

"It's nothing, really. We're glad to have you." I've had time to think, and now I mean this sincerely.

In the evening we go to see Miss Campbell and Mr. Phillips, bringing them some fresh-baked goods. They've never met Salahuddin.

Salahuddin and Mr. Phillips shake hands warmly.

"It's very nice to meet you, Mr. Phillips," Salahuddin says. "I've heard so much about you."

"And I've heard about you, too. Your mother could have been one of those little girls I saw when I was over there. It's a beautiful country."

Ramadan is over for another year. Yusuf fasted every day, and Sadeq got the CD player he's been wanting for Eid. There's no peace yet, but I'll keep on praying.

CHAPTER TWENTY-ONE

Lingering Concerns

THE WORLD DOESN'T break out in peace at the end of Ramadan, but I feel more peaceful. Since September 11 I have felt constantly tense and under pressure. Now, I think that I may be able to face the world again.

We face some problems that have nothing to do with terrorism. In late January the entire Midwest is hit with an ice storm. We have slick streets, broken branches and two days off from school, but we still escape the worst of it. I hear that in some cities people are without electricity. A week passes, and I hear that it's still not on in some parts of the Midwest. I don't want to do without my toaster and microwave for even a day, much less a week.

Sooner or later, everything thaws out. But the first days of spring are rainy and dreary. During these months of late winter and early spring, I ache for the California sunshine. A phone call to my mother in late March deepens my yearnings.

"You need to come out for a visit, Sally. It's a beautiful day today, warm and sunny. Do you still have all that ice out there?"

"No, Mom, that thawed out about a month ago. Now it's cold and rainy."

"I don't know why you and Salahuddin even bother living in a place like that. Wouldn't you rather just come out here and enjoy our beautiful weather?"

We like it here because the pace is slower and the people are friendlier. I've had this discussion with my mom before. "Well, once it gets warm it won't be so bad."

"I guess, if you're willing to put up with all that cold. Why don't you and the boys just fly out here for a few days, then?"

I still don't want to fly. I didn't like flying before the attacks, and now I'm terrified. For some reason, I don't feel comfortable telling my mother this. "Maybe we'll just wait until the summer and drive out," I say.

"Oh, that's a good idea, too. You can escape all that dreadful Midwestern heat and humidity."

I do miss the San Diego weather. But we like the people here, and this our home.

After a few more weeks of cold, the grass finally starts to turn green and the buds on the trees become flowers and leaves. The birds sing in the morning and my roses start to bloom. The fall and winter were long and full of difficulties. I hope that spring will fulfill its promise of a new beginning for life.

Terrorism is still very much in the news, of course. There are frequent news stories about suspicious characters, always with Arabic names, and our local paper runs a daily one-page section with updates on the "war on terror." There is still a general fear, too, that another attack could occur at any time.

One April evening during dinner Sadeq raises a different fear. "I was talking to this one guy at the masjid, and he said they might start putting Muslims into camps."

"Sadeq," says Salahuddin, "I told you before not to listen to him. He is far too radical, and paranoid as well. He probably thinks there are government agents hiding under our beds."

"No," Sadeq replies, "not the agents themselves. Just their bugging equipment."

"Last summer I put a jar of lightning bugs under my bed," says Amin. "Remember, Mom?"

"Yes, I remember. Sadeq is talking about something else, though."

"Yeah," says Muhammad. "He thinks they're listening to us through little microphones."

"Right now?" asks Yusuf.

"Could be," says Sadeq.

"La la la," Yusuf sings. "Do you like that, guys?" He yells into the air.

"That's enough," says Salahuddin. "'They' are not bugging us. You boys have to be careful who you listen to. Some people are extremists."

"Maybe they're right, though," says Sadeq. "Anyway, they did it to the Japanese, so they could do it to the Muslims, too."

"What did they do to the Japanese?" Yusuf asks. "Did they bug them?"

"No," says Sadeq, "it was worse. We've been talking about it in social studies. After the Japanese attacked Pearl Harbor, Americans were afraid that the Japanese people who lived in the U.S. would help the Japanese government attack other places, like maybe California. So the government rounded them up, took them away from their homes and put them all in big camps. Br. Imran said that over one hundred thousand Japanese were put in the camps, and most of them were U.S. citizens!"

"That's a lot of people," says Yusuf. "Are they still in the camps?"

"No, that was a long time ago. After a few years they got to leave, but by then they had lost their homes."

"That's not fair," says Adam. He's been listening quietly, with his head down, pushing his food around the plate. "They won't do that to us, will they?" he asks in a soft voice.

"No, they won't," Salahuddin says. "The American people learned from the mistake of the Japanese internment. They won't do it again."

"I don't know," says Sadeq. "The guy at the masjid said that the camps have already been built. He said they're going to stage another terrorist attack, blame it on the Muslims and put us all into camps."

"That's enough," says Salahuddin. "You will not be allowed to talk to him any more. I do not want him putting all types of ideas into your head."

"But, Baba," Sadeq protests, "what if he's right? What do you think, Mom?"

I've been listening silently to the discussion. Maryam and I were just talking about this a few days ago. Maryam, like Salahuddin, thinks that some Muslims are just over reacting, or maybe even trying to stir up trouble. I'm not so sure, though.

"Well," I start slowly, "camps are one way of controlling people. The Germans used camps to control the Jews, along with many others who opposed the Nazi regime. And the U.S. government did imprison the Japanese during World War II. Sometimes, I am afraid that it could happen again. Some Americans are very angry and distrustful of anyone who reminds them of the attacks." Salahuddin is frowning. "At the same time, most Americans are reasonable people who won't let their emotions get in the way. I hope that the peaceful and reasonable among us won't let the others get carried away. It could happen," I conclude, "but I don't think it will."

"Exactly," says Salahuddin. "From now on I will make sure you don't talk to that brother when we go to the masjid. He has dangerous ways of thinking. No good can come from it."

"But, Baba ..." Sadeq is cut off by a stern glance from his father.

We finish eating our dinner, and the matter is dropped.

Two days later, though, it is resurrected. Sr. Zainab calls in mid-morning, just as I'm about to head out for the library.

"Assalaamu alaikum, Sr. Sadia. I wonder if you could meet with me this afternoon. I've had some trouble with Yusuf."

"Yes, of course. What kind of trouble?"

"I'll talk with you this afternoon."

It must not be too serious, or the principal would have called. I think Yusuf's been doing all his homework. Maybe he got into an argument with Khalid, or talked too much in class. Oh, well. I'll find out this afternoon.

At the library I check out a book on conspiracy theories. I know Sadeq believes in them. I don't, really, but I want to know what all the fuss is about.

Sr. Zainab is waiting for me in the front hall when I arrive at school. We walk together to the conference room. Yusuf is already sitting at the table.

"I try to help my students explore new concepts, Sr. Sadia. I probably give them too much freedom in this aspect. Unfortunately, Yusuf has been coming to class with ideas that are totally unacceptable."

"What is it? What did he say?"

"Tell your mother why you're here, Yusuf."

"I don't know. I just asked a few questions, and she got all mad at me and everything."

"What kind of questions did you ask, Yusuf?"

"You know how Sadeq was talking about concentration camps the other day. I asked Sr. Zainab about it. I mean, she's the teacher so she should know."

Sr. Zainab speaks. "Yusuf scared his classmates. He asked me if it was true that all Muslims will be sent to concentration camps to live. A few of the children went home crying. I don't know your older son very well, but he seems to be a bad influence on Yusuf."

When I spent that day in the classroom with Sr. Zainab, she seemed so nice. "Sadeq is not a bad influence, and I resent that suggestion. He is a young man trying to find answers in these difficult times. Don't you allow the children freedom of speech in your class?"

"Of course I do, but Yusuf was out of line. Three mothers called me last night, wanting to know what kind of garbage I was teaching. One little girl had to stay home today because she kept having nightmares. We just can't allow this in our school."

I glance at Yusuf. He's listening intently, waiting for his mother to let his teacher know who's boss. "Yusuf, would you please wait out in the hall? I need to talk with your teacher privately." He walks reluctantly to the door. "And, Yusuf, please close the door."

I wait a moment to make sure Yusuf is out of earshot. "Sr. Zainab, Yusuf is a curious ten-year-old. His brother raised an important question at the dinner table on Tuesday night, and we discussed it. Did you consider discussing the issue with your class?"

"I have so much to teach those children. We don't have time for discussions, especially not over such ridiculous issues as concentration camps for Muslims."

"Well, I think you need to make time for discussions. It's a great way for children to learn."

"I'm the teacher, and I'll decide how they should learn. You need to have better control over your sons. Next time I'll take it to the principal."

I don't trust myself to say anything else. I know how hard teaching is, and I don't want to make things more difficult, even for a difficult teacher.

"Thank you for your advice, Sr. Zainab. Assalaamu alaikum." I walk out of the room, closing the door — maybe a little too forcefully — behind me.

Yusuf is waiting outside. "So, Mom, did you yell at Sr. Zainab?"

"No, Yusuf, I would never yell at your teacher. She works very hard to help you learn. I do think, in the future, it would be better not to ask those kinds of questions in the classroom."

"Oh," he says. He drags his feet the rest of the way to the car.

This is wrong, but I don't know what else to do. Yusuf is finding out at a young age that school is not always the best place to ask questions.

CHAPTER TWENTY-TWO

Back Home

WE STRUGGLE ON.

Yusuf makes it through the rest of the school year without controversy. At the end of the year Sr. Zainab reports, "Yusuf has been a very good boy."

I want to tell her that she took away his spirit. I doubt that she'll listen, though. Anyway, I know that the sixth grade teacher, Sr. Hafsa, inspires her student through creativity and caring. Summer vacation and Sr. Hafsa should revive Yusuf's spirits.

Spring is almost over, and the days are warm and humid. School is out and the boys are home. My days of quiet are on hold.

Muhammad is a high school graduate. He's received letters of acceptance from two universities — the local university that I want him to attend, and the one that's two hundred miles away. He still wants to leave home. We've sat down and talked with Salahuddin about it, but he refused to take sides. I think he wants to let Muhammad leave, but he knows how much I want him to stay. We have a few more weeks before Muhammad has to decide. Okay, he's decided already. I guess it's up to me.

Maryam and Musa drop by on the first day of June. When they pull up, I'm out in the front yard, pulling weeds. Their car is packed. She's excited.

"They just called. She's late, but the doctor said it could be any time now. She's been having a lot of small contractions. I hope we make it down in time."

"Drive carefully." I hug her. "Give Laila a hug from me, too. How long do you think you'll be gone?"

"After that little girl makes her appearance, we'll probably stay for a few more weeks. Laila's going to need some rest, and I can help little Yahya get used to being a big brother."

"Well, you'd better get going. You don't want to miss the little one's debut. I'll see you in about a month then, Grandma."

Maryam's laughing as she gets back in the car. Musa waves and drives off. I stand in the driveway, alone with my boys and my weeds.

June passes quickly, with slurpees, picnics, garage sales and yard work. In my spare time, I hang out with Khadijah and Asma. We go shopping together a few times, and sometimes just meet for tea.

On a Tuesday afternoon at the end of June we're having lunch at Asma's house. She laughs as she recounts her latest struggle with car repairs.

"A few months ago I didn't know anything about cars. But do you know that I can change my own oil now? It was messy, you should have seen it. I'm glad I wore some old clothes. But I did it. I'm so proud of myself."

"You should be," I say. "I could never change the oil in my car. Salahuddin just takes it into the shop."

"My father made sure I could do things on my own," says Khadijah. "He taught me how to change the oil, fix a flat tire and even do simple plumbing. He didn't want me to have to rely on a man to do things for me."

"I keep forgetting that you're from a different generation," I say. "When I was younger, I wanted to learn those things, but it still wasn't considered proper. My high school wouldn't even let girls take shop class."

"You're kidding. I didn't know things were so backward in this country."

"Like in my country, especially my family," says Asma.

"Back home my mother taught the girls how to cook and my father taught the boys about everything else. It was unthinkable to them that my sisters and I should learn to fix cars or that my brothers should have to cook and clean. Some of the men in my country love to cook, but never in my family. Uthman had those same ideas, of course. It's just since he's been gone that I've had to get by on my own."

"Well, I think you've done a good job," I say.

"Oh, I didn't tell you. I've decided to go back to teaching next year. I already talked with the principal. I'll be so happy to be back in the classroom. I missed the children."

"They'll be happy to have you back, I'm sure." I don't want to say anything about Sr. Zainab. She tried her best. But it will be good to have Asma back in the school. In a few more years she'll be teaching Amin.

Farhia comes into the room. Interrupting our conversation, she speaks in an urgent tone. "Mama, you need to come to the phone. It's Baba."

Asma's smile disappears. She seems frozen. It's a moment before she speaks again. "Baba?"

"Yes, come quickly. He needs to talk to you."

Khadijah and I sit silently on the couch while Asma goes to her bedroom to take the call. It's Uthman. I wonder where he is. Is he calling to say that he's coming home?

The living room clock ticks loudly, but time seems to stop. I don't know if she's on the phone for five minutes or an hour. Khadijah and I sit silently, waiting and hoping.

When Asma comes out of her bedroom, her children are all waiting by the door. "Mama?" says Aliya. "What is it? What did he say?"

The color is drained from Asma's face. Tears roll down her cheeks. She opens her mouth, but no words come out. She simply shakes her head and walks weakly down the hall back to the living room, finally collapsing in the forest green recliner.

Her daughters surround her, comforting her once again. Maybe I should leave. I glance at Khadijah. She's watching the scene intently, as if it's a play up on the stage. I guess she wants to stay. I guess I will, too.

We wait for several minutes more, frozen in the drama. Asma's daughters tend to her, bringing water and tissue. Farhia and Hakima are also crying. Fareed stands off to one side, staring into space.

Aliya tries again. "What did he say, Mama? When is he coming home?"

Asma stares into the empty space in front of her and begins to speak. Her voice is flat, without emotion. "Tomorrow he will be put on a plane, along with some other men, to be sent back to Pakistan. They won't let him stay here. They won't let him come home. He must go back to Pakistan." She pauses, and sighs deeply. When she speaks again, it's with tears in her voice. "He said that he loves you all and misses you very much He wants us to come to Pakistan, too."

Now all of her daughters are crying. I'm crying, too.

Asma kisses and hugs all her daughters. Then she calls to Fareed, who comes to her reluctantly. His shoulders are slouching as he drags his feet across the carpet. He stands uncertainly at the recliner, until his mother pulls him close. He cries for a moment, then pulls away and walks quickly to his room.

"Baba asked me to kiss all of you for him. He misses you so much."

"I miss him, too, Mama," says Aliya, "I really do. But I don't want to go back to Pakistan. I have one more year to finish my degree. Then there's medical school. What would I do in Pakistan? Get married?"

"But we have to see Baba," says Hakima.

"I wonder how he looks," says Farhia. "Did he tell you how they've been treating him?"

"No, we didn't talk about that. He sounds good, but he also sounds sad and quiet. I think he's changed."

Asma's changed, too. Will she be able to go back? I search

for the right words to say, but can't think of anything that won't come out sounding trite. "At least you know where he is, and that he's safe."

"Yes," she says, "at least that." She's calmer now. Her mind must be racing, though.

We sit silently for a few minutes longer before I excuse myself. "Well, I've got to get home now. Let me know if you need anything, Asma."

She walks me to the door and gives me the customary hug. "I will. Don't worry, I'll be okay."

I think she will.

CHAPTER TWENTY-THREE

A Business Trip

ASMA HAS A lot to think about, but I do think she'll manage. She's stronger, now, than I've ever seen her. Even stronger than when Uthman was home. She'll be okay.

For the last few days I've been worried about my own husband. Salahuddin is flying to New York this weekend to attend the annual conference for Muslim small business owners. He goes every year, and in past years he's come back with some good ideas for the restaurant. This year, though, I'm very nervous about his trip. I talked with him about it over a month ago, when he was filling out the registration form.

"You know, you could skip it this year. You still have your monthly meetings with business owners here in town. And the restaurant has been doing well. You don't really have to go to New York."

"What's wrong, Sadia? You never had trouble with me going before."

"Well, I'll miss you."

"I'll miss you, too. But this conference is important."

"There will be other conferences."

"Why don't you want me to go?"

"Okay, I don't want you to fly. Especially not to New York."

"Why not?" He paused. "Oh, I understand. It's because of the attacks, isn't it?"

"Well, yes. But aren't you worried? It could happen again."

"Do you remember that Saturday after the attacks when you just had to get out of the house? I think you said something about how if you didn't go out then, you might never get out. What about me, Sadia? Am I supposed to stay off of planes or avoid New York? For how long? If I don't go now, then when?"

He's got me. I wish his memory wasn't so good.

So he'll be leaving in three more days. He'll fly out with Ali on Friday morning and get back sometime Sunday afternoon. People fly every day, and there haven't been any more plane crashes in all these months. I need to stop worrying.

I call Asma on Wednesday. Uthman's plane took off in the morning, and he's on his way to Pakistan. She sounds calm.

"I miss him so much. But our lives are here. I don't know what to do."

I wish I could help her, but I don't know what I'd do in her place, either.

Salahuddin drives my little green car to the airport early Friday morning. I kiss him as he heads out the door.

"Don't worry," he says. "I'll see you on Sunday, insha Allah."

I am worried. All week I've had a nagging fear. "Sure," I say. "Have a good trip."

His flight should arrive by 11 a.m. our time. All morning I listen to the radio, bracing myself for the breaking news bulletin about a plane crash. It never comes. At 12 the phone rings.

"Assalaamu alaikum. See, I told you there was nothing to worry about."

No, I guess there wasn't. "I guess you're right." But I still have that nagging fear.

I take the boys out for pizza in the evening. Salahuddin has been in this country for twenty-five years, but he still doesn't like pizza. To him, it's not a meal unless it includes rice. Once, he even ate rice with spaghetti.

Saturday is normal. Muhammad and Sadeq have to work in the afternoon. I take the younger boys to the library and the nursing home. Fareed comes with us.

I'd like to ask Fareed how he feels, but I don't want to make him uncomfortable. I do listen to part of his conversation with Adam on our way to the library.

"My dad's in Pakistan now. He called yesterday from my uncle's house."

"When can he come back?"

"Never. They deported him. He has to stay in Pakistan."

"Are you going to see him?"

"I don't know. I want to see him, but they don't even play basketball in Pakistan. All they know is soccer, and I don't know nothing about playing soccer."

In a time of crisis you can think of the strangest things.

I have to pick up Muhammad and Sadeq from work on Saturday night because our other car is at the airport. I get Muhammad first.

"How was work today?"

"It was okay." His usual answer.

He looks upset. Don't ask me how I know. Just eighteen years of motherhood, I guess. "Did somebody give you a problem?"

"No, I said everything was okay." A little tense this time.

"What's wrong, Muhammad?"

"It's you, okay? I mean, I told you last summer that I wanted to go away. And you were all supportive and everything. Then, after the attacks you said you wanted to keep me at home. But I got accepted at the university, and I thought maybe you'd change your mind. I've got to let them know, Mom. If I don't decide soon, I could lose my spot. Why won't you let me go?"

It's too late in the day for tough questions. "I don't know, Muhammad. Everything's been so crazy this year. Just give me another week or so, okay?"

"That's what you always say." He sulks the rest of the way home, not even greeting Sadeq when he gets into the van.

I don't know why I can't decide. I don't know why I can't let him go. When I go to bed, I sleep uneasily with my nagging fear.

On Sunday I wake up tired, but excited. Salahuddin will be coming back, and I can put an end to this nagging fear. His flight should be coming in at about 3 p.m. I piddle around the house, keeping the radio on for that breaking news bulletin. Muhammad and Sadeq go to work, and the younger boys play ball in the back yard. It's almost 3 when the phone rings.

"Assalaamu alaikum, girl. How you doing?"

"Maryam. When did you get back?"

"Last night. Are you free? I've got to tell you about my little grandbaby."

"I'm just waiting for Salahuddin to get back. He went to New York for a conference. So, tell me about her." Maybe it will help if I think about something else.

"They named her Sakeena. She is the cutest thing you ever saw, every bit as cute as her brother. She's got her daddy's eyes, and Laila's mouth. I'm not kidding, either. That girl can wake up the whole neighborhood when she screams. But she is so sweet."

We talk for about thirty minutes. All the time I have one ear on the radio, listening for that breaking news. And the nagging fear won't go away.

Maryam would be happy to keep on talking, and normally so would I. But I've got to go. I have to concentrate on Salahuddin coming home safely. I try to sound casual, but my stomach is fluttering.

"Well, I've got to go now, Maryam. Salahuddin should be home soon."

"Okay, girl. I'll catch you later."

Salahuddin's plane should have landed by now. It will take him fifteen minutes or so to get his luggage, and another forty-five minutes to drive home from the airport. There were no plane crashes, and he should be home soon.

So why do I feel so anxious?

I try to read, but can't concentrate. I turn on the TV, but all I can find are baseball games, golf tournaments and infomercials. Wait, there's a movie. I recognize this. It's a Spencer Tracy movie, and I love Spencer Tracy. I think it's called "Test Pilot." Oh, I remember. There's a plane crash in this movie. Maybe I'll just go outside with the boys.

I go outside for a few minutes, but decide I'll feel more comfortable inside. I turn on the TV and watch the golf tournament. At least it's not violent.

I didn't sleep well last night, and I'm starting to get drowsy. I've almost dozed off when the doorbell rings.

Salahuddin's home, at last. I wonder why he rang the bell. He should have his key. I walk calmly to the door, and open it wide with a big smile on my face.

It's Ali. And I don't have a scarf on. I shut the door, run to put on a scarf and, red-faced, open the door again. Ali's eyes are focused on the blue planter on the front porch. Maybe he didn't notice.

"Assalaamu alaikum, Sadia."

"Walaikum assalaam. If you need to talk with Salahuddin, he hasn't come back from the airport yet. I'm expecting him any minute, though."

"No, Sadia, I need to talk with you. I was traveling with Salahuddin. We were scheduled to leave New York together this morning, but something went wrong at the gate." He pauses.

"At the gate? What happened?"

"Salahuddin was detained at the airport. They didn't say why. All I know is that they took him into custody. He won't be coming home today."

"What? Salahuddin? Why on earth would they detain him?"

"They didn't say. They just wouldn't let him on the flight. The screeners at the gate called security guards, who took him away."

"Salahuddin? Why him?"

"Security is very tight. I'm sure it's just some kind of misunderstanding. But from the look on their faces, I don't think they'll be letting him go anywhere for now."

I'm silent. Speechless, actually. We stand there awkwardly for a moment.

"Do you need anything?"

"Um, no, I guess not. No, Ali, thank you for coming by. We'll be okay, insha Allah."

"Salahuddin asked me to tell you not to worry. Are you sure you don't need anything? I could send my wife over to help."

"No, that's okay. Thank you."

"At least I'll contact Yaqub. He'll be able to take care of the restaurant while Salahuddin's gone."

"Yes, thank you. That would be good."

"Just call me if you need anything. Assalaamu alaikum." He turns and walks back to his car.

"Walaikum assalaam." I close the door slowly.

Salahuddin? This doesn't make sense. Maybe he forgot and packed a nail clipper in his carry-on. Would that be enough to hold him, to make him miss his flight? Nothing makes any sense these days, I guess.

I need to talk to someone. Ali's wife is nice, and I'm sure she would come right over, but she's not the one I want to see right now. I call Maryam.

"Assalaamu alaikum, girl. Did you get your husband settled in yet?"

"No." I stop, unable for a moment to say more.

"Sadia, are you still there? What's going on?"

"He, he's not coming home today. He's been detained. In New York. Ali came and told me."

Now it's Maryam's turn to be silent. When she does speak, she says only, "Salahuddin?"

"I know. Salahuddin?" I pause. "Maryam, could you come over?"

"Girl, I'm already there."

Five minutes later she's at my door. She hugs me, and that's when I cry.

"What am I going to do, Maryam?"

"You know Salahuddin. It's probably just some old nail clipper or something."

"But they may keep him for months, like Uthman. I try not to think about Uthman's deportation, but it keeps running through my mind. I just, I just don't know."

"Let's go sit down in the kitchen, and I'll make you some tea."

"Salahuddin, of all people. He's never even had a parking ticket."

"That's right. That's why you've got to stay positive. Now let's go get some tea."

We're walking through the living room on the way to the kitchen. The TV is still on, and I hear the words "breaking news." Even though I know Salahuddin won't be in a plane crash, I stop.

The newscaster looks somber. "We have just learned that a local man has been detained at a New York airport on suspicion of links to a terrorist organization. Early reports indicate that Salahuddin Abdullah may be part of a larger sleeper cell. We will have more details in our regular broadcast at 5."

It's a good thing that Maryam is there to catch me when I fall.

CHAPTER TWENTY-FOUR

A Safe Haven

OUR BOYS STILL don't know what's happened to their father, but now the whole town knows.

The phone rings about thirty minute after the bulletin. Maybe it's Salahuddin, telling me he'll be on a later flight tonight. He'll come home, and we'll sit and laugh about his nail-clipper adventure.

"Assalaamu alaikum."

It isn't Salahuddin. A strange male voice says, "Don't you know how to speak English? You foreigners need to get out of here, or we'll burn you out." He says some other things, too, before I slam down the phone.

"What is it, Sadia?" Maryam asks. Then she sees my shaking hands and pale face. "They've started already."

The phone rings again ten minutes later. Maryam answers, and quickly hangs up. Ten minutes pass, and the phone rings again. We ignore it.

"That's it. You and the boys are coming to my house. Call Muhammad to pick up Sadeq and meet you there."

"What if Salahuddin calls?"

"I don't think he will, not tonight. Anyway, you and the boys need to go where you're safe."

I call Adam, Yusuf and Amin in from their play. Amin is filthy.

"I was building a city in the dirt, Mom. It was fun."

I smile weakly. "Yes, I can see. Now, there's something I have to tell you."

"What, Mom?" asks Yusuf.

I wait a moment to gather my thoughts. I have to stay calm.

"I need you boys to get cleaned up. We're going over to Sr. Maryam's house tonight."

"Will we be back here when Baba gets home?" asks Adam.

This is the hard part. "Baba's not coming back tonight. He has to stay in New York a little longer. Anyway, Sr. Maryam has asked us to spend the night at her house. Won't that be fun?"

"Do we have to sleep there?" asks Amin.

"Yes, it's going to be an adventure."

He whines. "But I want to sleep in my own bed."

"It's just for one night, Amin. Now, go get washed up and change your clothes. Sr. Maryam is waiting for us to get ready."

As usual, the other two run off and Adam lingers behind. "Mom, why did Baba stay in New York?"

I don't like lying to my children. But Adam gets upset so easily anyway, it's no good making him more anxious. "He just has some business to take care of, that's all."

"Okay." I don't know if he believes me, but he does go off with his brothers.

While they get ready, I call Muhammad at work.

"Mom, I'm glad you called. I've been worried about you. I tried to call a few minutes ago, but there was no answer." Good, it was him and not that awful man. "My manager told me what they said about Baba on the news. What's going on?"

"I don't know. Br. Ali came by and said your father had been detained. Br. Ali was there when it happened, but he didn't know why they kept Baba. I just want to let you know that we'll be staying at Sr. Maryam's house tonight. I don't want to stay here. Some people have already called the house, saying terrible things."

"So that's why you didn't answer."

"Yes. Now I want you to pick up Sadeq and come to Sr.

Maryam's house. Ask your manager if you can get off a little early."

"Can't I just come home?"

"Muhammad, you didn't hear that phone call. I'll feel safer being with friends tonight."

"That guy who called is probably too much of a coward to do anything. Guys like him are just full of crap."

"Maybe, but ... oh, just come to Maryam's house."

"But what if somebody does try something? Sadeq and I could be there to protect the house, or in case Baba calls. Besides, I need to get my stuff."

"Just sleep in your clothes. You do that anyway half the time. I want to see you and your brother at Maryam's house within the hour."

"Okay, we'll be there." He pauses. "Don't worry, Mom. It'll be okay."

I smile briefly, in spite of myself. Is it the high school diploma that's making him more mature?

Maryam has spare guest rooms that she keeps for visiting children and grandchildren. She puts Adam, Yusuf and Amin in a children's bedroom fully stocked with book and toys. The boys become involved with these and seem to forget about home.

Muhammad and Sadeq come soon after we arrive. Maryam gives them bedding and directs them to the couches in the family room downstairs.

"Is that the room with the big screen TV?" asks Sadeq.

"Your father's stuck in New York and you're thinking about that TV. Boy, you've still got some growing up to do."

"Yeah, you're right. I'm sorry," he says.

"Just remember to say a prayer for him tonight."

"I will." We all will.

After the boys get settled in, Maryam sits with me in her kitchen. She gets me that cup of tea, and we talk quietly. She must be tired, but she stays with me until I start to yawn.

"Go ahead and get some sleep now. We'll take care of things in the morning."

I go into her adult guest bedroom. It's beautifully decorated in light shades of green and yellow, but the colors don't cheer me tonight. Salahuddin is being held somewhere in New York City, far away from us. I hope they treat him well.

CHAPTER TWENTY-FIVE

The Boys and Br. Musa

MY SLEEP IS filled with troubled dreams. I'm being pursued by the nagging fear. I can't see it, but I know it's there. No matter how far or how fast I run, it's right behind me. I don't know what will happen if it catches me, but I know that I have to keep on running.

In the middle of my dreams I hear crying. It sounds like Amin. Is he lost? Did the fear overtake him? I have to get to him. I have to.

I wake up. I'm not in my room and, for a moment, I'm not sure where I am. There is still crying outside the door. I have to go.

It is Amin. He's wandering up and down the hallway, probably looking for the bathroom. He's almost never been away from home and isn't used to waking up in a strange place.

"Come on, Amin, honey. The bathroom's over here."

He whimpers and briefly resists my guiding hands. It takes me several minutes to get him into the bathroom and safely back to bed.

"It's okay, Amin. Just go back to sleep."

He falls asleep instantly. But now I'm awake, and not eager to sleep.

I close the door softly. Maryam comes up from behind me and puts her arm around my shoulder. I jump.

"I didn't mean to scare you. Need some company?"

"Oh, Maryam, I'm sorry. Did Amin's crying wake you?"

"I couldn't sleep anyway. Let's go talk."

We go to the kitchen for more tea. Maryam brings out a chocolate cake and some cookies.

"As long as we can't sleep, we might as well try to enjoy ourselves."

I tell her about the nagging fear that has pursued me for the past week.

"I know that feeling. It stayed with me all those nights when Musa was out on the streets in Detroit. But we got through it. You will, too."

We sit and talk and eat for the next two hours.

"I'm worried about the boys. I haven't even told the younger ones about their father yet. I hate lying to them, but I don't want to get them all upset if it does turn out to be just a silly nail clipper. Soon I am going to have to tell them."

"Do you want me to help?" The voice is Musa's.

"Oh, Musa, I'm sorry. I didn't want to wake you."

"I had to get up. It's time for Fajr. Do you want me to haul those big boys of yours over to the masjid?"

"I didn't know it was that late. Yes, if you could, please. They're hard to get up, though."

"We'll see about that." He rouses them with his deep voice. "Salatul Fajr" is all he says.

A few minutes later Muhammad, Sadeq and Yusuf are racing through the kitchen on their way to the car. Adam trails slowly behind. "I don't know how you did that. They drive Salahuddin to distraction every morning."

"I've had lots of experience." He walks out the back door to join the boys.

We stop talking long enough to say our prayers. When they return, we're back at the kitchen table. Musa walks in slowly, behind the boys.

"You two don't ever stop talking, do you?"

Maryam laughs. "No sir, I guess we don't."

"By the way, Sadia, don't tell the boys about their father yet. Let's see what we can find out first. There's no sense worrying them if we don't have to."

"I think you're right. I'll wait, for now."

He looks around. "Now where did those boys of yours run off to?"

"I guess they went back to bed. They like to sleep again after Fajr."

"Not in my house they won't. I've got some yard work for them to do. You spoil those boys. I'll have a talk with Salahuddin when he gets back."

Musa calls for each of the boys by name, all except for little Amin, who is still asleep. Again, a few minutes later, they're all walking through the kitchen with Musa close behind. They're going to learn about work in this house.

"Musa is so good with the boys. I guess that's why your sons turned out so well."

"Neither one of us believed much in spoiling the kids, though Laila had it a little softer."

"What makes Musa so strong? Was it the trouble he got into when he was young?"

"No, it goes back further than that. He became the man of the family when he was just eleven and his own daddy was taken away."

"What happened?"

"The Klan showed up one night. They took Musa's father out to some woods and beat him till they thought he was dead. Musa found him the next day and got him back to the house. He lived, but he was never the same. It was up to Musa to keep the family going. He earned enough money to keep his younger brothers and sisters in school. Then, when he was almost sixteen, he got in with the wrong crowd. But Islam straightened him out. He got his G.E.D. and put himself right. By the time I met him he was pretty much the man he is today, just younger and skinnier."

"He's a very strong man."

"That he is. And we've got to get moving. My strong man likes a big breakfast after he's been out working in the yard. Then we'll get over to the masjid to see what we can do for your man."

* * * * *

Musa and the boys go right back out to work after breakfast. Maryam and I go to the masjid. The imam greets us.

"Assalaamu alaikum sisters. Sr. Sadia, I've heard about your family's situation. Do you have any more word about your husband?"

"No I don't, and I'm worried. Sr. Asma had to wait nine months, just to hear that her husband was being deported."

"Yes, she's had a very hard time. The climate was different then, right after the attacks. There was so much fear, I don't think Uthman ever had a chance of being released. I think that things are better now."

I hope so.

"Is there anything that my wife or I can do for you and your sons?"

"We'll be okay. Sr. Maryam asked us to come stay with her, and Br. Musa is helping out with the boys. So what should I do now?"

"I've already contacted some brothers in New York. They had talked with Salahuddin at the conference, and were shocked to learn what had happened. They'll try to get more information and see what can be done."

We talk for a while longer before going back to Musa and the boys. The imam will do his best, with the connections he has, to help Salahuddin. I don't know if it will be enough.

When we get back, they're all still out working in the yard. All except for Amin, who's playing in the dirt.

"Amin, come here. I want you to take a bath before lunch."

"But I'm not finished playing."

"Let's go."

I get Amin in the bathtub, then go to help Maryam fix lunch. We talk as we chop vegetables for the salad.

"So, what do you think I should do now?"

"Just give it another day or so. Hopefully the brothers in New York will be able to get to the bottom of this."

"I need to be getting back to my house."

"No, you and the boys are going to stay right here until your husband gets home."

"But I don't want to impose."

"You just stay and let us take care of you a little while. According to the hadith, you're allowed to be a guest for three days. After that, I guess we'll just have to throw you out!"

* * * * *

After lunch Musa takes all the boys to the masjid for the early afternoon prayer. Maryam and I pray together at the house. My mind wanders as I pray, and I think of my husband. I don't think he'll be able to go to the masjid. I hope they let him perform his prayers.

We hear the car pull up in the driveway. Muhammad and Sadeq come into the house first.

"We saw Yaqub at the masjid, Mom," says Muhammad. "He said that business is really bad today. Brett and Saleh came in, but that's about it. Reverend Wilson told Yaqub that people don't want to come to the restaurant because they're afraid of supporting terrorism. Most of the workers went home. Yaqub said that if Baba doesn't come home soon, he may have to close the restaurant."

"And Adam's acting weird, too," says Sadeq. "Weirder than usual, I mean."

"What's he doing?"

"Just crying and stuff. Don't ask me why. Br. Musa's talking to him, though."

"Maybe I should go out there. Adam might need me."

"The boy's almost thirteen," says Maryam. "Let Musa handle it."

She's right, I guess. I stay inside and watch them through the kitchen window.

After several minutes, they walk into the house together. I look at Adam. "Are you okay?"

His reply is harsh. "You lied to me, Mom."

"What?"

"He was talking to a brother at the masjid," says Musa.

"Yeah," says Yusuf, "the one Baba told Sadeq not to talk to."

"The man asked Adam if his father was still in jail. Not only that, he told the boys that their father will probably be deported, just like Uthman."

"Why did you lie to me, Mom?"

"I'm sorry, Adam. I thought it was the best thing at the time. I thought that Baba would be home soon, and I didn't want to get you upset."

"Is he right? Is Baba going to be deported?"

"Adam, you know that your father isn't a terrorist."

"Fareed said his father wasn't a terrorist, either."

I don't know what to say. Fortunately Musa steps in.

"Adam, we already talked about this in the car. Your dad is a good man. Sometimes bad things happen to good men. My father was a good man, too."

"What happened to your father?" asks Yusuf.

"One night some bad people came to our house and took my father away. They hurt him real badly. I found him the next day, brought him home and fixed him up. But that's when I realized that just being good doesn't stop someone from getting hurt."

"Are they hurting our dad?"

"No, they're not. I'm sure of it. They just need to ask him some questions. The point is, I had to step in and take care of my family. Can you do that, Adam? Can you help take care of your family while your dad's gone?"

"I guess I can."

"Do you know why bad things happen, Adam? It's a test. Allah is testing us to see how strong we are. We can cry or get angry, but that doesn't do any good. I've seen lots of men who got angry and ended up in prison because their anger got the best of them. It's no good at all. We can get angry, or we can work to keep doing good."

"How? What should we do?"

"Right now you can start by being good to your mama. That's first. Then, you can help your little brothers. And you can pray. You need to pray and ask Allah to help your dad, and to bring him home soon. Can you do that?"

"Yes, I think so."

"Good. No more anger, okay? And I want you to apologize to your mother."

"I'm sorry, Mom." He hugs me, and kisses me on the cheek. He's up to my nose now. I hadn't noticed how much he's been growing.

"So Baba really is in prison," says Yusuf. "Cool."

"I don't think it's cool," says Amin.

"No, it's not," says Musa. "Not at all. I want you boys to remember that. And now, I need more help in my yard. Let's get going."

Sadeq starts to groan, but a glance from Musa is all it takes to make him head back outside without complaining.

When they're all outside again I look at Maryam. "Your husband is really something."

She smiles. "Yes, I think so, too."

The rest of the day passes quickly and uneventfully. I think of Salahuddin every few minutes and say small prayers for him throughout the day.

During dinner Musa rubs his lower back. "Those boys of yours are good, Sadia, but they sure keep an old man busy."

"I'm sorry. Were they too much trouble?"

"No, not really. In fact, those big boys did a lot of things I've been meaning to get around to."

"One of these days," says Maryam.

"Something like that. Little Amin is something else, though. He is one active little boy."

Amin grins. He had to take a second bath before dinner. We're just finishing dinner when the phone rings.

"I'll answer it," says Musa. He listens for a moment, then hands the phone to me. "The imam wants to talk to you."

I wonder what he wants. "Assalaamu alaikum."

"Walaikum assalaam, Sadia. I have good news from New York. They're going to drop the charges against Salahuddin. He'll be on a plane home tomorrow, insha Allah."

"Are you sure?"

"Yes. They said he'll be heading out on an early morning flight, and he should be here by eleven."

I can breathe again, for the first time in two days. "Thank you," is all I can say.

"I didn't really do anything. I'm sure you're anxious to tell the boys. I'll see you at the airport tomorrow."

I hang up reluctantly, not wanting to separate myself from the bearer of good news. Maryam smiles. "So, what's the word?"

I can barely speak. "He'll be home tomorrow."

"Yes!" says Muhammad. He gives Sadeq a high-five.

Amin yells, "Baba's coming home!"

"Allah listened to my prayers," says Adam.

"Yes, he did," says Musa.

"But why did they arrest him in the first place?" asks Yusuf.

I don't know, but it doesn't matter any more. "I guess we'll find out tomorrow."

CHAPTER TWENTY-SIX

Peace

IT WILL TAKE a long time for the boys to settle down tonight. I'm not sure I'll be able to sleep, either.

I thought about going back home, but Maryam persuaded me to stay another night.

"You can get a good rest here, and we'll all drive out to the airport tomorrow."

"But we've been enough trouble already."

"I like having you here. We're usually so busy, it's been nice spending some real time together. Besides, most of the people around here still think that Salahuddin is a terrorist. What if the phone calls start again?"

"I guess you're right." I do send Muhammad and Sadeq to check on the house, and get a change of clothing.

"How is it?" I ask when they return.

"Everything's fine," says Muhammad, "except you left the television on. I told you those guys are cowards."

Yes, the brave people are the ones whose house I'm staying in.

It takes a while, but the boys do finally get to sleep. I'm so excited, I don't think I'll be able to fall asleep. But soon after my head hits the pillow, I'm drifting, floating pleasantly into a place of peace. I haven't felt peace like this since September tenth.

We leave for the airport at ten. We all go together in the van. Musa and Maryam have offered to drive my little green car back from the airport, so that our family can be together on the drive back. Earlier, Maryam put a pot roast in her crock pot. "You're all coming over here for lunch. No argument."

The plane arrives on time. Several people I know have come to greet Salahuddin, including Imran and Khadijah, and Asma and her family. A news crew is also here. They ran a story on the morning news about Salahuddin's release, and they want to show pictures of the happy reunion. That should put an end to the phone calls.

While we wait for the plane, I talk with Asma. "It was nice of you to come. It must be hard for you, though."

"You were there for me all those months, and I want to be here for you. At least now I can talk to my husband. He called this morning, and sent his salaams to Salahuddin and you."

"Have you decided what you're going to do?"

"Not quite. I've lived here for so long, it's hard to just pick up and leave. But I need to be with my husband. My oldest brother keeps telling me to just drop everything and come. He doesn't understand that it's not that easy."

No, it's not. I guess nothing really is. "I'm sure you'll make the right decision."

Finally, the plane lands and taxis up to the gate. "It's Baba's plane," says Amin. "He's here!"

Soon the passengers are coming through the gate. There's a grandmother, a group of teenagers and a young mother with two small children. I hope Salahuddin made the flight. Maybe they changed their minds, and we just haven't been notified yet. Maybe the imam was wrong. Maybe …

It's Salahuddin. He's walking slowly behind a young couple. He looks tired, and I think he has another gray hair.

"I see him," says Yusuf. "Baba, here we are!"

Salahuddin smiles broadly. His pace quickens. He passes the young couple, the grandmother and even the teenagers. The next few minutes are a flurry of hugs and kisses. "I missed you all so much," Salahuddin says as he hugs us each again.

Our friends wait patiently to greet him. "I feel like a celebrity," he says, as he shakes hands with Musa, Imran and the imam. The reporter approaches him for a comment. "I'd just like to say I'm happy to be home."

"How was your ordeal? Are you angry about your false imprisonment?"

"I'm happy to be home."

"Baba," says Amin, "did you bring us anything?"

"As a matter of fact, I did. I bought it before, well, before I went to the airport. I think everything is still in the my suitcase. Let's get home and we'll see what I have for you."

I drive the van back from the airport while Salahuddin catches up with the boys. It's been only a few days, but it seems like a month.

"Baba, they said that you're a terrorist," says Yusuf.

"That's what they thought, for a little while. It took us some time to get it straightened out."

"So you're not living some kind of double life then?" asks Sadeq. He's grinning.

"With you and your brothers to take care of, where would I find time for a double life?"

We go to Maryam and Musa's house first. In the van I've told Salahuddin about their kindness. As soon as I park in front of their house, Salahuddin gets out and walks over to Musa.

"Thank you for taking care of my family."

"I know you'd do the same." They hug. "Just watch out for that little Amin. He's a firecracker."

During lunch Salahuddin explains the reason for his detention. "First of all, my first name was spelled wrong on the ticket. It said 'Saladin.' They didn't catch it here in town, but it put up a red flag in New York. Because of that, they ran my name through the computer. It turns out that there is a Salahuddin Ahmed Abdullah from Indonesia who is on their list of suspected terrorists. I had to convince them that I'm Salahuddin Ahmad Abdullah from Singapore, and that I'm not on anybody's list. Some of the members of the Islamic community there helped me get it straightened out."

"Man," says Sadeq, "all that trouble over a little spelling difference."

"Well, they do have to be careful, I guess."

"Your mother's right. This whole country has suffered greatly because of the attacks. People are more fearful, and there are no guarantees that it couldn't happen again."

"How long will people be afraid?" asks Adam.

"I don't know. It could take a long time. I will tell you one thing. There are some people in the world who make it difficult for the rest of us. I have no idea who the other Salahuddin is. He could be a terrorist, or just another innocent man. But I want to remind you boys to be the kind of person who makes things easier for others, not the kind of person who makes things harder. If some Muslims do commit terrorist acts, it makes life that much more difficult for the rest of us."

That pretty much sums up the last several months.

* * * * *

After lunch we thank Maryam and Musa again, and head home. I let Muhammad drive my car so I can ride with Salahuddin. It is so good to have him back.

When we pull into our driveway, Mrs. Robinson waves from her front yard, where she's trimming her bushes. As we get out of the car, she comes over.

"I think it's just terrible what they were saying about you, Mr. Abdullah. I'm so glad that it was all just a big mistake. You've been such nice neighbors all these years. I just wanted to say that I'm glad you're back."

"Thank you, Mrs. Robinson." She's been such a nice neighbor, too. I'll have to bake her some cookies later. I know she has a weakness for ginger snaps.

My mother calls in the evening. She sounds worried. "I was talking to Amanda yesterday, and she was telling me about her niece. You know the one who lives about fifty miles from where you are? Anyway, she called Amanda yesterday and said she heard something about Salahuddin on the news. I told her she must have heard wrong, because she was saying that he's some kind of terrorist. What in the world is going on out there?"

I've been worried enough these last few days, and I didn't want to worry my mother. I'd forgotten about Amanda's niece. "He had a little problem coming back from his conference in New York, but he's home now and everything's fine. It was just a case of mistaken identity."

"That's good. I've been trying to call you for the last two days. I was starting to get concerned."

"You know Salahuddin, Mom. He could never be a terrorist. He has too much self-control."

"That's kind of what I told Amanda, but you know how she is. Anyway, I'm glad that everything's okay. So, when are you coming out. I can't wait to see those boys again."

There's been so much going on lately that I'd forgotten about going out to California. But I did promise, and I do want to see my mother. Besides, it will be a nice family road trip before Muhammad starts college.

"I don't know yet, Mom. Let me talk with Salahuddin, and I'll get back to you."

Salahuddin and I discuss it the next day. We decide that he needs to stay here in town, to work on building up the business. Even with the positive news reports, some people associate him with terrorism now. He'll have to work hard to rebuild his reputation.

"Why don't we leave in about two weeks?" I suggest at dinner that night. "Then we can be back in time for Muhammad to get ready for college."

"Which college?" he asks warily.

"Well, I think you showed a lot of maturity when your dad was gone, so you're probably ready to go away to school. What do you think, Baba?"

"I think that Muhammad is a man now, and we need to

let him go where he thinks he'll get the best education. So, if you really want to, Muhammad, you can go."

"Yes!"

He is a man. But he's still my first baby. I'm starting to miss him already.

CHAPTER TWENTY-SEVEN

The Anniversary

AMIN IS KNOCKING on my bedroom door. "Mom, I can't find my book bag."

"Just a minute, Amin. I'm getting dressed."

"But I need my book bag."

"Be patient. I'm coming."

I look at myself once more in the mirror. Yes, I look good.

I finish dressing and open the bedroom door. Amin is still there.

"Mom, I can't find my book bag."

"Did you look on the blue chair in your room? It's probably underneath something."

"Okay, I'll look." He goes off on his search.

On my way down the hall I find Sadeq standing outside the bathroom door.

"Mom, can you tell Adam to hurry up? He's been in there for about an hour already."

Adam has started caring more about his appearance lately, but I doubt he's been in there that long. "Adam, hurry up. Your brothers have to use the bathroom, too."

Before I reach the stairs Amin comes out of his room, book bag in hand. "You were right, Mom. Thanks."

The kitchen is quiet. Salahuddin is almost finished eating breakfast. I pour myself a cup of coffee. "I can't believe it's been a year."

"It's been some year, too," he says.

"Yeah, what with arrests, terror alerts and the restaurant almost closing."

"We're making it, though. We'll get through it."

Yes, we are making it.

"Where are those boys of yours?" he asks. "We need to get to school."

"Well, the last time I checked, Adam was in the bathroom and Sadeq was waiting for him to finish. Amin was heading downstairs with his book bag." I stop to do some mental math. Who's missing? "Yusuf. Has anyone seen Yusuf yet this morning?"

"No," says Salahuddin, "but you need to make sure he's up and ready. That Yusuf has been late every day since school started this year. He used to be so good at getting up."

That was before his growth spurt.

"Yusuf." I call up the stairs. Sadeq is still waiting in the hall. "Sadeq, have you seen Yusuf yet this morning?"

Adam finally emerges from the bathroom. Sadeq calls down, "He's probably still asleep, but I can't get him. I've got to get ready." He disappears into the bathroom.

Never mind, I'll do it.

This all seems so familiar. As soon as I get one kid all ironed out, I've got another one ready to give me the same problems. Well, I guess they'll all be grown soon. I might even miss these days.

Finally Adam and Amin are in the car, and Sadeq is headed down the steps, running toward the front door. Salahuddin honks the horn several times. Yusuf runs downstairs, dressed but barefoot.

"Be sure to borrow Sadeq's comb and brush your hair in the car." I don't know if he hears me as he slams the front door.

Now it's my turn. I finish my coffee and a bagel. This time I know the interview will go well. A year ago, I wasn't ready. I probably would have messed it up. After everything we've been through this last year, though, I feel more confident. I know I can do the work.

I put on my dark green scarf, grab my keys and head

out to my car. As I drive, I think of the little blue engine. But I don't just think I can, I know it.

I walk in. The secretary asks me to wait for a moment, then escorts me into a somewhat larger office. A middle-aged man with thinning brown hair sits behind a desk that is cluttered with papers.

"Hello, Mrs. Abdullah, I'm glad to meet you. My name is John Watson. You may call me John." He extends his hand.

"And you may call me Sally. But I'm sorry, I don't shake hands with men."

"Oh, excuse me. There's so much to learn. I think people have been learning a lot about one another over the past year."

"Yes, I agree."

The interview goes smoothly. Mr. Watson, I mean John, asks me about my experiences and seems genuinely inter-ested in the talents I've gained as the mother of five. Along with the conventional questions about salary and work hours, I ask him about the children at the center. It feels like a pleasant conversation, not the interrogation I had imagined.

At the end of the interview I expect the usual reply, that he will contact me and let me know, the old "don't call us, we'll call you" routine. Instead, he says, "Sally, I think you'll work out very well here at our facility. I'm impressed with your ability to communicate, and I think you will be a great help to our children here. Could you start on Monday?"

Yes, of course, I can't believe it. I don't shake hands with men, but I feel like hugging you. "Yes, John, I can do that. I look forward to working here."

"We'll look for you on Monday, then."

It's a home for emotionally disturbed children. I'll be doing some tutoring and organizing some activities for the children. If I take some more college classes, I can become a counselor. I'll talk with Salahuddin about it later.

When I get home, I call Maryam.

"Hey, girl, what's the news?"

"I got the job."

"I knew you would."

"I'm so excited. Those children need so much attention. But I think I'm up to it."

"I know you are."

We talk for a while longer. Ahmad is being transferred to Chicago, so he'll be closer now. Ibrahim and his family will be coming for a visit in a few more weeks. Laila is doing fine. She's decided to quit her job at the end of the year and stay home with her two children. "And she's so much calmer now, even with another little one to take care of."

"It was the pregnancy hormones. Most pregnant women are crazy, at least part of the time." I know I was.

"So how's your college student?"

"Muhammad seems to be doing well. He likes his classes, and he really enjoys meeting new people. He'll be coming home next weekend, probably with dirty laundry."

"Yes, I remember those days. Ahmad never did his laundry at college. He would save it all up until he came home. I don't know how that boy ever had enough clean clothes to wear."

"Well, I've got to start cleaning up around here and think about dinner. Talk to you later."

Before deciding on what to cook, I go to check the mail. There's a letter from Asma.

"Assalaamu alaikum. We made it back here without any problems. We're still getting settled in. Poor Fareed doesn't know much Urdu, so he's having a rough time. The girls and I always spoke Urdu when we worked around the house together, so they're having an easier time adapting. My oldest brother has been telling them that they need to get married soon. Fatima likes the idea, but Hakima says she's not ready for marriage yet. She wants to come back to the U.S. to study.

"I miss Aliya and Farhia, but they needed to stay and finish their education. They like living with their uncle in Kansas City. They say that people are very friendly there. Aliya will start applying to medical schools soon. She has good grades, so she should be able to get in. I'm not sure what Farhia wants to do after graduation. She says she might want to come back to Pakistan for a year before deciding on graduate school.

"I made the right decision in coming back. It's good to be a family again. Uthman was in good shape when I came because our relatives have been working to fatten him up. I can tell you that it's working.

"Please give my salaams to everyone there. I hope to see you again someday. Of course, you're always welcome to come see us in Islamabad."

I hope I can, someday.

As I mix the spices for the chicken, I think about the past year. It hasn't been easy for anyone, but I know I've grown. I wonder how my life would be if the attacks hadn't happened.

Now they're saying that there could be a war in Iraq. That makes me nervous. We don't need any more wars. Khadijah, who gets most of her news from the internet, tells me that the war in Afghanistan isn't finished yet. I hope there will be an end to all this fighting soon.

A year ago today, it is said, nineteen Muslim men hijacked and destroyed four airplanes, in horrific acts that caused the deaths of almost three thousand people. According to the reports, they were acting under the banner of Islam. That, supposedly, was their jihad.

For the past year I have struggled to wear my scarf, keep my independence, protect my family and help my friends. We almost lost the restaurant, and for a few days I thought I had lost my husband.

We're stronger now. I wear my scarf without apology, I'm able to let Muhammad live far away from home, and I

177

have a new job. The restaurant is thriving again. My husband is stronger, too, for his ordeal.

It hasn't always been easy, but I'm making it. This is my jihad.

GLOSSARY OF ISLAMIC TERMS

All Muslims, regardless of nationality, use certain Arabic terms to express different Islamic ideas and practices. These are the terms used by Sadia and her friends and family.

Allah: Allah is the proper term used by Muslims to refer to the Supreme Being. Muslims believe that Allah is the Creator and Ruler of the universe.

adhan: The call to prayer, always recited in Arabic. The message of the adhan is: Allah is the Greatest, There is no god but Allah, Muhammad is the messenger of Allah, Come to prayer, Come to victory.

alhamdulillah: "All praise belongs to Allah". Muslims use this phrase in a variety of situations, often expressing gratitude or relief.

Assalaamu alaikum: "Peace be with you." This is a common greeting among Muslims, and is dictated by the teachings of the Qur'an. The proper response is, "Walaikum assalaam", or "peace be with you, too."

Br. or Sr.: Stand for "brother" or "sister." Muslims commonly refer to one another in this way. This denotes the unity of the Muslim community.

Eid: Literally, a festival. There are two Eids during the year. Eid'l Fitr comes at the end of Ramadan. Eid'l Adha comes at the end of the annual pilgrimage to Mecca.

Eid Mubarak: A common greeting on Eid day, it means "Blessed Eid."

Five Daily Prayers: Muslims pray five times each day. The prayers and their times are: Fajr (between dawn and sunrise); Dhuhr (shortly after noon); Asr (late afternoon); Maghrib (early evening); Isha (at night).

imam: A Muslim leader.

insha Allah: Literally, "if Allah wills". Muslims say this with the recognition that nothing can happen if Allah does not allow it.

Islam: The religion that Muslims practice. This word means both "submission" and "peace."

jihad: Struggle in the cause of Allah. Under certain circumstances, this can include military warfare. A wider meaning of jihad is any effort to do something that is pleasing to Allah, even raising children in the proper manner.

masjid: The Arabic word for mosque, the place of congregational worship for Muslims.

Muslim: A Muslim is a person who practices the religion of Islam.

Prophet Muhammad: Prophet Muhammad is recognized by Muslims as the last in a long line of prophets sent by Allah. Muslims work to follow his example.

Qur'an: The holy book of Islam, the Qur'an is believed to have been revealed from Allah to Prophet Muhammad through the angel Jibril (Gabriel).

Ramadan: The month, on the Arabic calendar, when the Qur'an was first revealed. Healthy adult Muslims must fast from dawn to dusk every day during this month.

suhur: The early morning meal eaten before dawn during the month of Ramadan.